BERNESE ADVENTURE

BERNESE ADVENTURE

by
JANE SHAW

TO

R. C. F. E.

PROLOGUE

"Though what your absurd school wants to go having an epidemic in the middle of April for, and throwing you on our hands for six weeks, I can't imagine." Mrs. Peter Storm addressed her daughter Sara and her niece Caroline in disgust. "Why at this time, of all times? Just when your poor father has decided at last to take his first decent holiday for years! If, even, Aunt Caroline and Uncle Gavin hadn't made up their minds to come to Norway with us, there would have been a home for you there; but now what are we to do with you? —our passages booked and both the houses to be shut up and everything—"

As she stopped for breath Sara and Caroline looked slightly guilty and felt that indeed the scarlet fever epidemic which they had greeted with such unholy and unsympathetic glee, was their fault entirely: although, as Sara nearly pointed out, it wasn't so much the epidemic as the school's sudden desire to heave up all the drains, which had sent them home for an extra holiday.

"Of course, it's very unfortunate that Vanessa and John should be going away for May, too," put in Caroline's mother, glancing at her elder daughter who was sitting with a far-away look on her face, as if not one word of this conversation were reaching her, "otherwise the girls could have gone to the flat for a month."

9

John—for the families were in full convocation
to discuss the fate of the girls, with the exception
of Sara's brothers, pursuing their studies normally
and more or less happily elsewhere—John said
quickly, in some alarm:

"Of course, we'd be delighted to have them in
the ordinary way, but you know I must put in an
appearance at this conference in Basle, we can't
possibly alter our arrangements now—"

"Oh, don't worry, John," laughed Sara's
mother, "we won't ask it of you. *I* know how
much you would enjoy housing Caroline and
Sara."

"I dare say I could find them a couple of spare
beds in the hospital," said Sara's father, who was a
surgeon, but neither Sara nor Caroline seemed to
consider this such a good joke as he did.

"We could take them with us," said Vanessa,
coming out of her trance. The look of incredulous
delight which lit the faces of Caroline and Sara
made an interesting contrast to the look of incredulous horror which lit the face of John.

"My dear Vanessa! Do you feel *capable,* apart
altogether from inclination, of escorting these two
maniacs half across Europe? Our ancient car, for
one thing, would never stand it—"

"No. No," said Vanessa in her vaguest voice,
"I think it would be absolute torture. But it would
get the parents out of a difficulty; and the poor
scraps must go somewhere, and nobody seems able
to shelter them."

The poor scraps exchanged a solemn, delighted
look and turned on John two pairs of eyes which

appeared as if their owners had suffered hardship and persecution since birth.

"Gertcha!" said John. "You can't come the pathetic over me like that. *I* know you. But," he went on, obviously weakening, "what do you think, Aunt Margaret? Would it be a help if we took them?"

With relief, Sara's mother answered, "My dears! I should just think it would! But it seems too bad for you and Vanessa to have your nice holiday spoiled—"

Sara spoke for the first time: "I can't think why every one should imagine we *would* spoil their holiday. Gosh, John, you'd have a marvellous time when we were about—adventures, capturing international jewel thieves and motor bandits or something—"

"That's just it," sighed John, and grinned at her. "I don't think I'm just so good at capturing international jewel thieves as I was. But meantime, why don't you two take yourselves off and have an adventure till we can decide your future without your disturbing presence?"

Caroline rose lazily from where she was lying, half buried in the sofa cushions.

"Come on, little shrimp," she said to Sara. "They want to talk about us behind our backs."

Sara showed a disposition to argue against leaving this most interesting discussion, but Caroline led her away. "Gosh, Caroline," she was saying before the door shut behind them, "d'you think they'll take us? *What* fun it would be—"

"Oh, they'll take us all right," answered Caroline calmly, closing the door, "or Vanessa wouldn't have put the idea into our heads at all. And, of course, the gorgeous bit is," she went on, "that the conference only lasts a couple of days or so, and after that they're going on to the Bernese Oberland."

"Where?" said Sara.

"You know, Interlaken or somewhere about there—mountains and mountains and mountains."

"Oh, lovely! I've always longed to go ski-ing."

"Ski-ing? You don't go to Switzerland in May for ski-ing. And maybe we don't go to Switzerland at all."

But they did: for that very evening it was decided that Sara and Caroline should go with Vanessa and John in their Morris Major car for a month's holiday in Switzerland—

"—and France and Belgium and Italy and Poland and Turkey," Sara, her desires getting the better of her accuracy, explained breathlessly to any of her friends who would listen.

CHAPTER ONE

IT was the week before departure and they were assembled in the Douglases' flat in Glasgow for another of the seemingly endless discussions. Caroline lay, apparently asleep, full length on the sofa, while Vanessa, with an anxious look on her face and a pencil in her hand, perched uncertainly on its edge; Sara was sitting on the floor, hugging her knees, and John sat, very business-like, at his writing-desk, with an official-looking black note-book before him and his pen poised.

"Now, look here, Sara," he was saying, "there's just one point: Vanessa and I are planning to do this trip as cheaply, *and* as interestingly, as possible, so you can get all ideas of big hotels and sumptuous meals right out of your head, and get used to the idea of lodging in small inns or private houses, for that should be both inexpensive and amusing."

Sara bade reluctant farewell to visions of herself lording it in luxurious Continental hotels, meeting the Arch-Duke This and bumping into Prince That while rescuing their priceless heirlooms from the hands of a bunch of crooks. They weren't new visions, but they had never seemed so near possible realisation before, and as they were rather nice, too, she listened to John with disgust as he went on:

"Vanessa, will you buy—in Woolworth's, if you can—a bread-board and knife—?"

"Yes, darling," Vanessa murmured. "But we have a bread-board, actually; maybe you've forgotten because we don't seem to use it much, but it has a sort of silver frill round it and it's really very nice. Somebody or other gave it to us for a wedding present—Mrs. Clutterbuck, I think—"

"No, no, Vanessa," said Caroline, "*she* gave you two of the sixteen toast-racks, don't you remember? Of course, I shouldn't wonder if you thanked her very prettily for a bread-board—"

"I didn't, I swear I didn't!" Vanessa became quite agitated. "I was most careful about all the thank-you letters—"

"So careful," Caroline jeered, "that you wrote old Miss Walkenshaw three times thanking her for an embroidered tea-cosy she hadn't sent—"

John interrupted; determined to be patient, but showing the effort. "You know," he said, "I don't want to spoil you girls' fun, but the idea of this meeting was rather to make decisions about the trip, not discuss an eighteen-month-old *gaffe* of Vanessa's."

"Well, you started it," said Sara, still disappointed in John, "breaking in with lists of household requirements—"

"My good girl, the bread-board and knife which I asked Vanessa to buy are destined to accompany us."

"Gosh! What for?" said Sara.

"Well, I intend that we shall have a picnic-lunch on the road, each day, and you've no idea what a boon a board and proper knife are when you're trying to cut a large loaf in the middle of a field," John answered.

The others gazed at him in amazement and admiration for this masterly attention to detail, and "B.-b. and k." went down on Vanessa's list.

"Now about clothes," John went on: "you must only take the absolute minimum. I shall get everything of mine into a rucksack, so will Vanessa, and you two will manage with one between you—or no, better take a small suitcase and then you'll have room for a grand suit for me to wear at the conference." Sara looked more than doubtful at this, and Caroline remarked that if they did manage with one case between them it would be a miracle, for they all knew what Sara's packing was like, didn't they?

"Besides," she went on, "she says she's going to take both a ski-ing outfit and bathing things."

"Well, well," said John, brushing aside these feminine and childish irrelevancies. "Don't you know it's May? Now, with reasonable luck, we'll do Glasgow to London in one day and save a hotel. Vanessa, have you written to make sure that half-witted cousin of yours is prepared to give us a bed for the Wednesday night?"

Vanessa looked guilty. "I'll do it to-night, John, I promise. Not that it matters much, really, for we'll have to sleep on the floor in any case, but I'll write and warn him."

"There you go, no help from any of you, every-thing left for me to do—"

"What exactly have you done, John?" said

Caroline lazily from the sofa. "Because it was Daddy, through me, who got the R.S.A.C. man on to triptyques and car-nets and insurance and arranged about the car ferry at Dover. All you do is sit back and give orders—"

"Well, naturally," John grinned, rubbing the side of his nose, a trick he had when amused. "I'm the brains of this expedition. You can't expect me, a busy man—*and* extra busy with correcting under-graduates' exam-papers—to go running about looking for triptyques. Besides, I put the G.B. plate on the car. And," he added proudly, "I got my photograph taken for my International Driving Licence—"

"Yes, darling, you've done very well," smiled Vanessa. "And now you're all ready—except for having your hair cut, of course—*don't* forget that, darling. Caroline will manage to get the rest of us off safely, I'm sure."

"*And* me," said Sara, eagerly. "I've been doing masses of things, and gosh, I'm *terribly* capable!" at which Caroline, with whom Sara had been doing the masses of things, laughed mirth-lessly.

"I don't suppose they'll go developing scarlet fever all over the Continong?" asked Vanessa suddenly. "For if they do I shall pack them straight home."

"Oh, gosh, *no!*" Sara was vehement about that dire possibility, which had been discussed in privacy by Caroline and herself.

"Apparently not," John corroborated. "They were never actually in contact with any cases, and if they *have* got it, Uncle Peter was telling me, they'll have time to develop it before we leave and we can cast them into a fever hospital."

"Callous creature," said Sara.

But, as seemed fairly certain from the report the two had brought back from the school doctor, no symptoms appeared, and on Wednesday, May 1st, they set off at, according to Caroline, a very inhuman hour; and, after an exhausting day's motoring with, according to Sara, far too infrequent stops for nourishment, they did reach London, and Chelsea, and found the half-witted cousin with beds made up all over his living-room floor, eight of them, some very primitive. For Caroline, knowing her sister, had written to him herself, asking him to house four people for the night, but never suspecting that Vanessa, belatedly mindful of her duties, would send a telegram just before leaving Glasgow with the same request.

"Well, I did feel it was a bit of an invasion," the poor young man confessed, "but I thought I'd better be on the safe side. And Mrs. Jones has cooked goodness knows how many pounds of sausages for supper—there are some potatoes, too, somewhere—just see if they're behind the sofa, Sara, will you?"

"I'm very fond of sausages," Sara confessed as she hunted for the potatoes. "Enough for eight people—what bliss!"

They discussed the next day's programme as they ate sausages and mash and drank coffee.

"Where are you going to, by the way?"

inquired the cousin, as he plied Sara with more and yet more sausages.

"Paris, Basle, Zurich, Geneva, Vienna, Budapest, Baghdad——" Sara reeled off the names ecstatically, like a person in a travel agency. The cousin looked suitably impressed, but Caroline said:

"Pipe down, Sara. Actually, we've decided— or they've decided," she corrected herself, jerking her head towards her sister and brother-in-law, "to go to Grindelwald ultimately—it's in Switzerland, in the Bernese Oberland, you know," she added kindly, in case her cousin's geography was something like Sara's. "Of course, we've to land John at Basle for his conference——"

"If you ask me," interrupted Sara, "there's something jolly fishy about those conferences which John and his old engineer pals are always getting up to—they happen in such nice places and at such suitable times. When the university's on vacation and he's not lecturing. I believe he invents them——"

"Any more unfounded suspicions from you, and I'll make you attend *all* sessions of this conference as my stenographer," threatened John.

"Oh, gosh!" said Sara, whose interest in engineering went no further than to know the fate of the plans of the new aeroplane stolen by the foreign spy recounted in every other book she read (the ones in between dealt with murders and robberies, with an occasional ghost thrown in). "What's a stenographer?"

"We cross by the Townsend Ferry," went on

Caroline, as soon as she could get a word in, "and the A.A. made us out a route, the quickest, to Paris first—"

"My good girl," interrupted John frigidly, "surely you're not trying to tell me that you expect me to follow a route that some ridiculous man sitting in a stuffy office has drawn up? Besides, it's the first I've heard of it."

"But John," said Caroline, "I told you Daddy had done that bit. And these A.A. people know all about the roads—"

"Nonsense!" John said sweepingly, "I know where I'm going. Vanessa and I went through France last year; and I want to have a look at Belgium; *and* I've no intention of going to Paris again."

"Oh!" said Caroline helplessly.

"Isn't that sickening?" Sara was wistful. "I'm longing to go to Paris. It was a nice route, too—Caro and I had a look at it—though it didn't go as far as Vienna."

"We'll make straight for Brussels," said John, glaring at her. "And I'll be obliged if you'll stop going on about Vienna, Sara—"

"But we must go to Vienna, because I've an uncle there, Uncle Thomas—" began Sara.

"Are you sure?" said Caroline. "I've never heard of an uncle in Vienna."

"Of course I'm sure," said Sara. "There's a cousin as well, Jane; and he's not your uncle, any-way. Just because our fathers are brothers doesn't mean we have all the same relations. I've a whole set you've nothing to do with at all—"

"Like me," said the cousin, helpfully.

"I know all that, fathead," said Caroline. "I only meant I'd never heard of your uncle Thomas."

"—so that's why we must go to Vienna," Sara finished.

"Sara," began John, going slightly purple.

"Well, well!" broke in the cousin in a bright voice. "Now *that's* settled," he hurried on, "what about to-morrow?"

"The Townsend Ferry leaves Dover at eleven-thirty," said John, "and we're requested to be there by eleven; so if we leave at nine-thirty—"

"Are you flying there?" the cousin queried with interest. "Or don't you know it's about eighty miles to Dover?"

John, who seemed suddenly to have developed a liver or something, was in one of his awkward moods, and wasn't listening to advice.

"Well," he said impatiently, "we can easily do it in a couple of hours."

"Honestly, John, that's cutting it rather fine," said Caroline, "and I don't think we *can* do it."

"Now that *would* be a pity," said Vanessa's gentle voice. "Do listen to Caroline, John darling, it's always safer."

"Leave it to me," said John grandly. "We'll be all right."

"Oh, gosh!" Sara, who disliked fast driving, groaned quietly to Caroline.

"Looks as though you're going to enjoy the drive to-morrow," replied Catherine sourly.

None of them did. John had apparently made up his mind to be obstinate, for he took his time getting up, and they didn't leave Chelsea till nine o'clock; then they got all mixed up on the outskirts of London and could not find the Dover road; and what with stopping for petrol and one thing and another, time was getting on at such a rate that even John noticed it. They hurtled through Kent, Sara with her eyes shut, and the luggage—there having been no time to strap it on—knocking her and Caroline to bits in the back seat; not to mention John's climbing boots, which he had brought without any regard to the season of the year.

"And if *you* had had your way," Caroline muttered rather savagely to Sara at one point, "we'd have skis to bang us about as well." Sara had nothing to say to this, but moaned slightly and kept her eyes shut; and the feeling in the car grew less and less friendly towards John, until, when they crashed on to the quay at Dover, to see the little ferry casting off, he had undoubtedly become the villain of the piece. They sat disconsolate, and watched the grinning faces of the people who had had the wits to catch the boat.

"That's the ferry, that was," at last giggled Sara, who was not unduly sensitive to atmosphere. Vanessa and Caroline were so busy not saying "I told you so" that the effort nearly chocked them.

"When's the next one?" asked Sara.

"To-morrow morning," said Caroline, with difficulty.

"Oh, gosh!" said Sara, disgustedly. "But it's rather funny," she continued, "to think that we nearly burst ourselves doing Glasgow to London in one day to avoid having stay in a hotel, and *then,* at the end of it, miss the ferry. Isn't it rather funny, John?"

"I say," interrupted Vanessa, creating a diversion, "I was at school with a girl who married a man in the army. I'm almost sure she lives here, and she'd love to have us stay—she's always inviting me to come and see her."

"I don't suppose you remember her name?" Caroline suggested.

"Yes, of course I do—Podger."

None of the others seemed to be so impressed with this feat of memory as Vanessa.

"What was the name of the man she married?" said Caroline patiently.

"Well, Podger always referred to him as Chinky—"

"Oh," said Sara, taking an interest, "is he Chinese?"

"Oh, I don't think so," said Vanessa, although this solemn thought hadn't struck her before. "Maybe he was born in China, or looks a bit yellow. But he must have another name, surely? I wonder what it could be—"

"I wonder," said Caroline.

"Don't be cheeky, Caroline," John said, taking command again. "Now, Vanessa, concentrate. We'll make for a telephone-box and get a directory, and meantime you concentrate, *hard.*"

Vanessa concentrated like anything, and by the time they had found a telephone box and a directory she had rejected about ten suggested names and decided that she was *almost* sure it was Smith. John ploughed through all the Smiths in the book, hoping the addresses would strike a chord; but at each one Vanessa shook her head.

"D'you know," she said, after they had been through them twice, "I'm beginning to think it couldn't be Smith after all." The other three sighed. "I've a feeling it was a more Scottish name than Smith. I've got it! Williams!"

"That's Welsh," said Caroline.

"Yes, so it is; but Williams is certainly the name."

"Doesn't matter if it's Greek," said John, turning to the Williams's. "Now we're getting somewhere."

"Yes, but John," said Vanessa guiltily, "there's another thing I've just remembered."

"Well, what is it?" John asked, looking up full of hope.

"I've just remembered they live at Aldershot," said Vanessa.

CHAPTER TWO

IT took Sara at least some little time to understand why they were now looking for a nice hotel, and to realise that poor Vanessa did not know and had never known any one who lived in Dover; but as she told Caroline in the seclusion of their bedroom later, The Three Bells was *very* nice, and she for one was jolly glad they weren't going to spend another night on somebody's floor: and as even John, for all his ingenuity, could not contrive that they should miss the ferry a second time, Friday morning saw them safely on board and very well pleased with the little boat, and particularly with the great claw arrangement that lifted the cars off the pier into the hold.

"Major Morris doesn't look so bad, does he?" said Sara as they watched the car dangling in mid-air.

"The luggage looks a bit odd," said Caroline. The Major was not new enough to have a boot, and the luggage, exposed as it was to public gaze, certainly did have a peculiar appearance. Sara, under dire threats from John, had agreed to one suitcase between herself and Caroline, but considered she had come well out of the lack of space difficulty by begging a very grand hogskin travelling bag from her father because it had soft, pliable sides and so was suited to her methods of packing. The recent gift of a grateful patient, it was meant for aeroplane

travel, and though Mr. Storm had never been in an
aeroplane in his life, and saw small chance of ever
being in one, he was inordinately proud of the bag
and only gave in to Sara's entreaties to borrow it
for peace's sake, and on condition that she treated
it with the greatest tenderness. So there it sat, on
Major Morris's rack, very new, very yellow, and
in marked contrast to the two filthy old haversacks
which surmounted it. John, outside the hotel that
morning, had already admitted that they weren't a
good idea. "It's *impossible* to strap these knobbly
brutes securely on," he raged—until the Boots
came to his rescue, or the whole party might have
been outside The Three Bells to this day.

When the cars were all aboard and the ferry left
the quay Vanessa and John wandered below, while
Caroline insisted that Sara should be properly
impressed by the white cliffs of Dover. Sara put on
her specs and snorted.

"Well, I don't care if they are famous," she
said, "I think they're mouldy. Come *on,* Caro,
let's look round for some crooks," she added,
hoping no doubt to further her consuming desire
for adventures, her favourite at the moment, in view
of all this foreign travel, being one in which she
found herself capturing—single-handed, or perhaps
with a little help from Caroline—gangs of spies or
like gentry and being thanked by a grateful
Government for saving Britain. It didn't depress
her at all that her life so far had been singularly
free from such excitements; something was bound
to happen one day, and it was best, she assured

Caroline, as she dragged her round the boat inspecting their fellow-passengers, to keep on the look-out.

"I hope the sea stays clam," was all Caroline had to say.

Sara was so busy looking over her shoulder at a foreign gentleman, with beard, whom she felt sure must be a spy, that she crashed into a tall, blonde woman who was walking peacefully round the deck, and sent flying out of her hand a book.

"Clumsy idiot!" muttered Caroline, as they all three dived to retrieve it.

"I'm most frightfully sorry," said Sara breathlessly, reaching it first and picking it up, glancing as she did so at its name. *"Tales of Mystery and Imagination,* is that a new one? It's a marvellous title—do you like mysteries—is it good?" She peppered the lady with questions and completely failed to notice, though Caroline did, that she had gone white under her make-up, that she almost grabbed the book from Sara and tucked it firmly under her arm, and that her face had a look of strain as she answered:

"Thank you so much. Yes, it's very good. Isn't it a lovely day?" She seemed in no mood for a literary discussion.

"Yes, it is," agreed Sara, easily side-tracked. "I hope it's like this all the time we're abroad."

The lady was only giving quarter of her attention to the girls, looking about the deck as she talked. "Yes," she said absently. "Are you going far?"

"Oh, rather!" said Sara eagerly. "We're going to Paris and Basle and Geneva and then to stay at Grindelwald, then maybe we're going on to Vienna and Budapest."

"That *will* be nice," said the lady. "Oh, there's my husband, will you excuse me?" And flashing a vague and brilliant smile at them she hurried away.

"I wish you wouldn't go talking to strangers, Sara," said Caroline. "You bore them. And I wish you wouldn't tell whoppers about where we're going—"

"Well, but, Caro, when we're at Grindelwald anyway it seems a pity not to go on to Vienna, and maybe if we talk enough about it John *will* go."

"Maybe John will strangle you if you mention Vienna and Budapest again," said Caroline. "She did get into a stew, didn't she?" she changed the subject.

"Who? What are you talking about?"

"That dame—"

"Oh, her! Wasn't she gorgeous-looking?"

"M'm! I suppose so. I didn't like her much."

"Didn't you, Caro? She was *beautiful."*

"Yes, I dare say. But she wasn't bothering about us at all when she talked to us, only about her old book. And she was a bit—flashy, somehow."

"Was she? I didn't notice. She has—"

"Shut up! She'll hear you if you bawl like that —she's just over there. And that's the husband, I suppose: they don't look very friendly, though, at the moment, do they?"

"Maybe they're deciding to part for ever," suggested Sara, with an eye to drama. If only Sara could have heard the conversation she could have made up a far better story than that; but by now there were more important things than the possible arguments of a rather flashy-looking couple to occupy their thoughts, as the girls hung over the side and watched Calais approach. They missed the shouting, blue-smocked porters they had seen the year before at St. Malo, but, after they had disembarked themselves, Sara got enough excitement out of trying to take a photograph of Major Morris being disembarked. Then there was the passport inspection, which Sara adored, although she was always trying to apologise for her passport photograph.

"Makes me look like a sick monkey," she declared crossly, whereas with her lively little face, short chestnut curls, and pointed ears, she looked more like a very healthy puck. Caroline, on the other hand, regular of feature and very fair, photographed beautifully, which annoyed Sara. However, to-day she didn't get much time to bother about passports, there was such a fuss going on. The cars were all lined up, and from where Major Morris was, far back in the queue, the girls could see the customs officials subjecting the front cars to the most close examination.

John was away coping with triptyques very gravely, with Vanessa's wifely assistance; and the girls, standing by the car, were giggling at all the strange little things they could find to giggle at, when, rather to their astonishment, their acquaintance of the book came over from her handsome yellow Armstrong-Siddeley coupé parked some way in front, and hung round Major Morris with them, chatting—about nothing, as Caroline remarked when she left them.

When it came to Major Morris's turn for examination two customs men set about the car very thoroughly. They lifted up cushions, they poked into pockets, they looked under the floor carpets, they shook the rugs: there was wild excitement when they came to John's boots.

"Quoi donc, qu'est-ce que c'est, qu'est-ce que c'est?" one of them, a little dark youngish man with bright, twinkling eyes, cried, lifting the right boot high in the air; his colleague had meantime grabbed the left one.

"Qu'est-ce que c'est, qu'est-ce que c'est?" he cried.

"Those are boots," said Sara helpfully, and, for all the world like terriers, they started to worry the boots.

"Isn't this examination extra rigorous?" mildly inquired John, who had reappeared, fearing they'd have the soles off his boots before they were done.

"They think your boots are stuffed with dope," giggled Caroline. Without a word the men, giving up hope of the boots, seized on the bread-board.

Sara was bursting with curiosity, so she put on her most winning expression and said, "Why are you being so thorough—are you looking for something?" It worked: the little lively one took a quick look round, then bending towards Sara whispered:

"In England last night there was a robbery, and a diamond necklace was stolen: it is worth thousands of francs! It is worth millions of francs!

It is priceless! And the English police think the thief he try to enter into France."

"No!" said Sara. "Oh, how absolutely thrilling—Caroline, d'you hear? Maybe the thief was actually on the boat! Maybe we actually saw him!"

The customs men by this time had decided that anyway it wasn't Sara, and that the priceless necklace wasn't in or about Major Morris, so the party, twittering over this excitement, were free to drive off.

"We got away quicker than some," John observed, nosing the Major out of the line of cars.

"These two are still going through it," said Caroline, nodding towards the yellow Armstrong. As they passed Sara gave a wave, and was rewarded by a look of complete amazement and horror from the flashy lady. Sara was vaguely surprised, but had other things to think about.

"John," she said. "John, we must buy a paper and see what it's all about. It's thanks to you, John, that we're in on this, for if you hadn't been so silly"—John made a grumbling noise but offered no remark—"we should have caught yesterday's ferry and missed all the fun. I want a paper."

"I want to see a group called, I think, 'The Burghers of Calais,'" said Vanessa. "It's by Rodin, and it should be somewhere about."

"I want some lunch," said Caroline.

John didn't say what he wanted, but when, after driving up and down innumerable side streets, he came to rest outside a quiet little restaurant called

—deliciously, they thought—*"Au Filet de Sole,"* it was obvious that he and Caroline were of one mind. He went in and ordered lunch, Vanessa dragged Caroline off to find her "Burghers of Calais," and Sara went to buy an English newspaper. She came back eventually, after the others, her eyes popping.

"It's in here," she said, as if that made the whole business seem real after all. "There's not much— I suppose the papers haven't had time to get details. Listen—" but she didn't have the chance to read it aloud before the others crowded round and hung over her and read for themselves:

VALUABLE JEWELS STOLEN

"Manridge Park, in Kent, the home of Mr. J. Johnston Phillimore, the millionaire shipowner whose hobby is the collection of unusual jewels, was the scene last night of a particularly daring robbery. Late at night or during the early hours of this morning a thief or thieves entered the house and removed the famous Phillimore Necklace. Mr. Phillimore's collection of gems, usually kept in safety in London, had been brought to Manridge Park to be inspected to-day by Heer Van Rooij, the great authority on diamonds, who had come over to England from Amsterdam specially to view the collection. The police are in possession of several important clues—"

"They always say that," snorted Sara, "when they're absolutely stumped. And here's a bit about

the necklace—took him twenty years to collect—
150 perfect stones, emerald cut, gosh! Then something about carats—that's not the way you spell
it—oh, I see!—well-known stones—difficulty of
finding a market in England—close watch being
kept on all ports—insured for £50,000! Well, isn't
this the most *thrilling* thing that could happen?"

"It *would* have been more thrilling if we had
seen the thief—and the necklace—being un-
masked," remarked Vanessa, truthfully enough.

"Sara would have burst a blood-vessel if she'd
seen either," said John. "Come along, children,"
he added, "we must get on. Eat up."

And the excitement of getting even so near as
they had done to a real, live crime certainly spoiled
no one's appetite.

CHAPTER THREE

MAJOR MORRIS left *"Au Filet de Sole,"* and was
heading cheerfully for Ostend with Sara, who
wanted to show off, urging John to remember to
drive on the right-hand side of the road.

"Sara," said John, to divert her, "is my hat
there?"

"Oh, you and your hat!" muttered Sara, grovel-
ling on the floor. "It's an awful-looking thing,
too. Vanessa, why did you let him bring such a—
gosh, what's this?" Sara, red of face from poking
on the Major's floor, sat back on her seat, staring at
a book she had picked up. It was a handsome book,

thickly and heavily bound in leather, and it was called *Tales of Mystery and Imagination*.

"I say," said Caroline, "that's Blondie's book—"

"So it is," said Sara; "how did it get here?" She flipped over the pages and came on a tiny bundle of English newspaper cuttings. "Hallo," she said, looking at them, "these are all about the robbery of the Phillimore necklace—why should she cut them out, I wonder?"

"Maybe knew Mr. Millionaire Phillimore, and was interested," suggested Caroline.

"Oh, *blow*!" Sara complained; "if we had only known!—we could have asked Blondie about it; maybe she would have given us the low-down on the whole thing!"

On the suggestion of John, who was finding the sun a bit hot, Vanessa turned round to discover why his hat wasn't forthcoming, and wanted to know what they were talking about.

"Well, it's this book," said Sara. "On the ferry I bumped into this Blondie person—did you notice her? Marvellous-looking, big and blonde, but Caroline thought she was flashy—anyway, I nearly knocked it into the sea—"

"Knocked Blondie into the sea?" said Vanessa in an amazed voice, thinking she ought to have heard of this sooner.

"Gosh, *no,* the *book*!—and I picked it up, and you should have seen how she grabbed it from me. And then we chatted for a bit—"

"Sara chatted," put in Caroline.

"—and here it is."

"Well, really, Sara darling, that's stealing, you know—"

"Gosh, Vanessa," Sara bounced up and down in her seat with rage, "I didn't *pinch* the thing, I gave it back to her—"

Vanessa glanced at the book in Sara's hand and then looked helplessly at Caroline, who told her all *she* knew about *Tales of Mystery*. "But," she finished, "I don't know how it got here, unless Sara borrowed it from her when we were talking on the quay."

Sara began again in a cross, excited voice to disclaim all knowledge of the beastly book when John interrupted patiently:

"I suppose that somewhere about Basle one of you two will remember to pass me my hat, to protect me from this hot sun—"

Caroline fished his hat out from among the rugs, boots, and maps on the floor, while Sara collapsed into her corner, muttering.

And as soon as they were settled again John ruined everything by asking, "Is the luggage all right?" and Sara and Caroline screwed themselves into uncomfortable positions from which they could catch a glimpse of the luggage-grid.

"Luggage all safe," Caroline reported. "Ow! But my head jolly well isn't—that's twice that bread-board's come down and hit me. Shove it over there on the floor, Sara."

"It hit me once," said Sara, "and nearly knocked my specs off." Sara's reluctance to wear her glasses was only balanced by an equal reluctance to miss anything. She seemed to have great hopes of this journey, for her glasses had scarcely left her nose since they set out from Glasgow.

"Not that there's anything much worth seeing in *Belgium,*" as Caroline said, but quietly, lest John should hear and get wild at her: "It's flat, and there's no scenery, nothing but fields, and the roads are awful."

"M'm! Seem to be composed of cobbles," said Sara wonderingly. "And gosh, I'm thirsty! *Gosh, I'm thirsty,*" she tried it rather louder, and John came to, and said:

"All right, all right; we'll want some petrol soon, too; we'll stop at the next combined petrol-pump and café, and we can all fill up."

"Yes, but John," Caroline said, "we haven't anything to buy petrol with."

"Neither we have," John agreed. "Now, isn't that a bore? I've got a beautiful supply of Swiss francs, but I shouldn't think the Belgians could make much use of them."

"Gosh!" said Sara. "Do we have to starve until we reach Switzerland? *And* I'm so thirsty—"

"Well, your throat will just have to crack, like mine," gloomed Caroline, "for we don't seem to have any money."

"Money?" Vanessa said. "I've got some French money."

"There you are," said John. "I think of everything. Caroline," he hurried on, "you'll have to do the talking; I—er—don't feel like speaking French to Belgians this afternoon."

"Oh, Sara can do that," said Caroline lazily.

Sara who, since she and Caroline had spent the previous summer in France, considered herself no end of a linguist, was only too pleased; so when they stopped at the next petrol-pump (having made sure there was a café as well), she greeted with confidence the plump young woman who came forth.

"Bonjour, Madame—"

"Better ask if she can speak French," interrupted Caroline.

"Gosh, what do you expect her to speak?" asked Sara.

"Flemish," said Caroline coldly.

"Oh!" said Sara. "Oh, gosh—this is going to be more difficult than I thought!" But yes, Madame could talk a little French; yes, Madame would accept French francs in exchange for some petrol—how many litres of petrol would Mademoiselle like?

"How many litres of petrol would you like, John?" Sara asked, delighted with the progress Madame and she were making.

"I want six gallons," said John uncompromisingly.

"Oh, gosh," said Sara, "how many litres are there in a gallon?"

Caroline thought there might be six, but then again there might be three point three repeating, you never could tell with these silly foreign measures; Vanessa was convinced, and kept telling every one of her conviction, that *litre* was the French for book and had absolutely nothing to do with petrol, but as it was seven years since she left school they weren't to rely on her too much, and John said firmly:

"Four and a half, near enough."

"You *are* clever!" said Sara. "So that means we want twenty litres—"

"Twenty-seven," murmured Caroline.

"Twenty-seven litres, please *Madame.* Gosh, that's pretty good order!"

Madame seemed to think so, too, and started to calculate the cost of the petrol. Translating so many Belgian francs per litre into so many French francs per gallon and then into honest English money to see what they were really paying, was a lengthy and involved calculation, as Madame and Sara did it, and the answer was only achieved by having resort to paper and pencil and the combined brains of Vanessa, Caroline, and John; so it was an exhausted party which finally trooped into the cafe and sat down at a table.

"What d'you want to drink, Sara?" asked John, giving his order to Madame, who had popped up again as the *patronne* of the cafe.

"I'll have cider," said Sara....

Afterwards they all piled into the car again, Vanessa driving.

"Sara," Caroline said, "I wish you'd stop scratching yourself. It's disgusting."

"I only wish I could," said Sara unhappily, rubbing herself up and down against the back of the seat.

"Is the cap on the petrol tank?" The discussion was interrupted by John from the front seat. After craning her neck nearly out of joint Sara announced it was.

"Is the luggage all right?" John asked, a mile farther on. Sara, after an altercation with Caroline, announced it was.

"Is my hat there?" said John, but not all the searching among the debris on the floor revealed John's hat; so, in spite of protests from Sara, who thought they should leave well alone, Vanessa turned the car and back they went to the cafe for John's hat.

CHAPTER FOUR

WHAT with the elusiveness of John's hat, and stopping for an evening meal, and one thing and another, it was ten o'clock before they reached Brussels, and found a little hotel, unpretentious enough to suit John, in a quiet street near the square. The proprietor had not been expecting guests so late but, he assured them, he had two beautiful rooms, all ready.

While the four were filling up the forms making themselves known to the authorities, Sara muttered to Caroline:

"I want to go to bed *now.* Come on."

Caroline was surprised. But the placidly acquiesced.

"What's biting you?" Caroline asked as they mounted the stairs.

"That's just the trouble," said Sara in a

worried voice: "I only hope it is something biting me."

Caroline looked a little vacant at this cryptic utterance, but the unfolding of Sara's worry was delayed by the discovery in their room of the proprietor himself, making up the beds.

Sara offered her assistance, which was thankfully accepted, for M. Jacquet certainly had not the air of an expert bed-maker, and, as he explained, the chamber-maid was having the evening off to go to the cinema. Sara taught him all she knew about bed-making, and in return he gave her, prompted by her questions, a quick summary of his life story. But at last he went and Sara removed her glasses and started tearing off her clothes.

"Caro!" she said: "I'm going crazy! I've been wanting to scratch all day and there must be something wrong with me! Oh, gosh, Caro! Look!" Sure enough, Sara's little chest and tummy were covered with angry red blotches.

"There are some on your back, too," said Caroline interestedly. Sara gazed with horror first at her reflection in the mirror, then at Caroline.

"I knew it," she said in a broken voice: "I've got scarlet fever."

This was a new idea to Caroline, who started; but she said briskly: "Rot! You can't have. Uncle peter said before we left that we were absolutely safe. Besides, no one in our house took it, and we were never with any of the people who did."

"I can't help that: I've got it," said Sara. "Besides, I feel awful."

"How d'you mean, awful?"

"Gosh, I don't know—just awful. I'm sure I've got a temperature."

Caroline, as she had seen her mother do, pressed her hand to Sara's forehead, not very clear as to what to expect, but thinking it looked helpful.

"Don't feel anything," she said. Sara groaned. "Oh, well," Caroline sighed, "I'd better go and fetch Vanessa."

"Stop, Caroline, you mustn't," Sara cried, catching hold of her cousin's skirt. "If it's scarlet fever we'll all be shut up in some frightful hospital and we'll probably die—"

"Well, but you certainly, can't wander all over Europe with scarlet fever," objected Caroline.

"No, but wait—you know what Vanessa said about sending us home, and that would be worse. And maybe after all I *haven't* got it: I'll see if I'm still spotty in the morning, and if I am, I'll ask M. Jacquet where there's a hospital and the doctor there'll tell me what's up. Vanessa would clap me into bed whether I had it or not, *or* send me home."

Caroline continued in her view that Sara was being unreasonable, and that Vanessa should be summoned at once, but finally she gave in to Sara's entreaties. "All right," she said, "we'll wait till the morning. And you can push your bed right into that corner and not come breathing over me."

Sara, feeling her position, and only too thankful for a night's grace, accepted this harshness as meekly as an outcast should.

"And don't scratch," counselled Caroline, undressing.

"No, Caroline," said Sara in a small voice,

creeping into bed and clawing herself unmercifully under cover of the bedclothes.

Caroline reluctantly awoke next morning with something soft hitting her on the face, to find Sara, fully dressed, shying stockings and bedroom-slippers at her from a safe distance.

"Wake up, Caroline," she was chanting in a voice of doom. "I've still got it. I've still got it."

"Got what, you fat idiot? And shut up throwing things at me. I'm awake."

"Scarlet fever," said Sara, shocked by such callousness into her natural tones.

"Oh, that!" muttered Caroline, rolling over and snuggling down into her pillows. "Go to sleep now, and tell me about it in the morning."

"It *is* morning," Sara said, dancing with impatience. "It's half-past seven, and I'm going to the hospital. And if you don't come with me, I'll go by myself. And maybe I'll collapse and die on the way, and then maybe you'll be sorry," she finished, nearly in tears at this pathetic picture. Caroline poked her chin out over the sheet and regarded her solemnly.

"*You'll* not die as easily as that," she said. "Oh, well," she sighed, "I'd better get up and look after you or they'll put you in a madhouse. But has it struck you, little shrimp, that if you go to this hospital, and you *have* got scarlet fever, they may not let you out?"

" 'Course they will. They won't want an infectious case in beside appendixes and things."

"I still think you'd be better telling Vanessa," argued Caroline as she washed.

"No," said Sara. "Not till I *know* for certain I've got it.

"Although I'm sure I have," she added, as they sought out the hospital, carefully following the directions given by M. Jacquet, rather astonished at the request, but hoodwinked and flattered by Sara's hastily concocted and mendacious story that she was very soon going to start studying medicine and wanted to see the famous hospitals of Belgium while she had the opportunity. "For I had the most ghastly night. Didn't sleep a wink."

"You must have gone deaf then," said Caroline, "for twice I bawled at you how were you feeling and—"

"Here's the hospital now," Sara interrupted quickly, and added importantly, "just follow me."

"You'd better ask someone," began Caroline.

"Ask someone? Gosh, no! I know all about hospitals. We'll make for the out–patient department—this is it, I expect, where this man's going." Sara bustled along in the wake of a tall, sturdy-looking Belgian.

"Just because you know your father's hospital, doesn't mean you know all about Belgian hospitals." said Caroline, who didn't seem to be in the best of tempers this morning. "And that man doesn't look much like a patient to me, in *or* out—"

Sara ignored her, and continued to follow the man, who, directed by a passing nurse, had disappeared through some swing doors. The girls,

close on his heels, found themselves in a large bleak
room with tiled walls and hard chairs ranged stiffly
round three sides. Four or five men and women
were sitting there, none of them, as Caroline took
care to point out to Sara, looking much in need of
medical aid. Before Sara could think of a crushing
answer a nurse came in by another door and summoned the young woman sitting first in the row.
One by one the people before Sara in the queue
went through the door, and Sara became more and
more nervous, suddenly regretting that she hadn't
enlisted Vanessa and John, and thinking now that
this hospital visit was one of the poorest ideas she'd
had for a while.

"I'm going to be sick," she whispered to Caroline. Caroline, knowing Sara's little peculiarity of
being sick when very much excited or nervous,
glanced at her rather anxiously, but said briskly, in
a low voice:

"Nonsense! You can't be sick here."

"Can't I?" said Sara, aggrieved. "It's a
hospital, isn't it? That's what a hospital's for, isn't
it, for sick people?" Caroline was spared the
necessity of replying to this by the reappearance of
the nurse or, as it now seemed to Sara, the horrible
ogre dressed up, who was saying, "Mademoiselle
will come now?" and holding open the door.

"Don't leave me," Sara said in an agony,
clutching Caroline.

Sara, in her excitement and because her glasses
were reposing in the hotel bedroom, saw nothing of
the room they entered, only a dapper little man in
a dazzling white coat who smiled at the girls

quickly and absently, and said "Good-morning, mesdemoiselles." Then he added, after a second glance. "You are surely very young?"

"Oh, not so very," said Sara, in her best French, and thinking she was old enough to have scarlet fever, anyway.

"Ah, you are brave!" said the doctor rather unexpectedly and certainly inaccurately. Sara, in face of this tribute, clutching her last poor remnants of courage before they left her entirely, opened her mouth to explain her symptoms, but to her horror, before she could get a word out, one of the nurses grabbed hold of her head, rubbed her ear with some strong antiseptic, the little doctor approached with a small but evil-looking instrument in his hand, put his hand on her head—and Sara's nerve gave way completely. With a yell she wrenched her head away and went flying out of the door before the astonished doctor could begin, as he obviously intended, to cut her throat.

"Ah, zut! What foolishness is this?" he said angrily. "What is the matter with Mademoiselle your friend?" he turned fiercely on Caroline.

She, who, for all her ignorance of hospital procedure, was thinking it was a pretty funny out-patient department which treated first and diagnosed after, considered it was time there were some explanations.

"We are English—" she began, in her lazy, drawling French, entirely innocent of French accent.

"English?" interrupted the doctor in surprise, while the nurses stared.

"On holiday," continued Caroline firmly, determined to be heard, "and my cousin did not feel very well, so we came to see a doctor——"

"Ah, *mon Dieu,*" the little doctor threw up his hands, "but my dear young lady, you have come to the wrong department! This is not for patients; here we——" and he launched into some explanation the only word of which Caroline could understand was "blood."

"Help!" she thought, "I'm getting out." But she outwardly remained her calm self, and smiled, and said, "I am sorry, but I do not understand. Can you tell me that in English?"

The doctor beamed self-consciously and shrugged one shoulder. "I only speak a very little English," he apologised in that language, "but I will try. Here we make the tests of blood. When we have a patient very ill and we need to make a blood—what do you call it?—translation?——"

"Transfusion?" suggested Caroline, rather pleased with her knowledge.

"Ah, yes, transfusion. Before that happens we make the tests to see who is suitable, so that when the time will come there will be a list of peoples in the proper grade who will be ready to give blood without delay. So we ask for volunteers to come to-day, and we test them."

"I see," said Caroline, grinning. "I'm so sorry we have been so silly. I'll go and find my cousin now and take her to the right place."

The little doctor smiled and bowed and shook hands with her (and told her how to find the out-patient department, quite on the other side of the building), and the nurses smiled, and Caroline smiled, and came out, wondering where Sara had got to by this time.

She found her, right outside at the entrance gates, lurking behind a big gate-post and peering out suspiciously, in a manner obviously of great interest to a policeman watching her from the other side of the street.

"Oh, there you are, Caro! I thought maybe they were going to murder you. I was awfully worried, darling, but I thought it wouldn't be any help to you if I came back and was murdered too—"

"Nice of you to worry, though," Caroline grinned at her.

"Oh, I *did*!" Sara assured her earnestly. "But how did you get away? What were they trying to do to us?"

"Nothing, you fathead. And come out from behind that gate—you look so daft. No, perhaps the next time you go to a hospital you'll not be so cocksure but condescend to ask the way instead of dragging me into the middle of a blood-test—"

"Oh, gosh, is that all?" said Sara, rather disappointed, now that the danger was over, to discover there never had been any. "Here, where are you off to, Caro?"

"The out-patient department, of course where d'you think? Come on, it's just over here," and Caroline began to walk in the direction the little doctor had indicated.

"Caroline!" Caroline stopped and turned round, rather surprised at the solemn tone of Sara's voice. "Caroline," said Sara, "you can go to out-patient departments till you drop, I'm going back to find Vanessa and John."

They found John in a very bad temper, marching up and down outside the hotel, and Vanessa, trying to soothe him and at the same time mildly concerned at their disappearance, trotting up and down beside him.

"Ha," said John, "so there you are! And where d'you think you've been? I knew what it would be—I warned you, Vanessa—I told you we'd never reach Switzerland with these two. Besides, we've been very upset, worried to death, wondering where you were, thinking you had been run over and taken off to hospital—"

Caroline giggled, which didn't improve matters, and while John took breath, glaring at her, she took the opportunity to say: "Run upstairs with Sara, Vanessa, will you? She has something to show you."

As Vanessa disappeared with an anxious, gabbling Sara, John concentrated his just wrath on Caroline.

"Now Vanessa's gone. 'Something to show her,' indeed! All this *would* happen just when I want to leave early. I planned to leave at nine, and it's long past ten o'clock now. Goodness knows when we'll get away—"

"I don't think we shall get away," said Caroline calmly.

"Not get away?" John stared at her. "What do you mean?"

"I think Sara has scarlet fever," said Caroline, disappearing into the hotel. She ran upstairs and into their bedroom, where she found Sara buttoning up her sweater and grinning all over her face, while Vanessa sat on the bed laughing at her.

"Oh, hallo, Caro darling!" Sara called. "Fancy, I haven't got scarlet fever at all—"

"No!" Caroline mocked her.

"No, it's nettle-rash. Vanessa says it's hay-fever, but I know about that, and I think she means nettle-rash; she had it once just after she was married."

"I expect it's from eating all those sausages," said Caroline severely.

"Gosh, I only had about two! Or maybe three," said Sara, "and sausages never gave me anything before."

"I don't suppose you ever ate so many at one sitting before," Caroline suggested.

Sara ignored this, and said, "What's the cure, Vanessa?"

"Cure?" said Vanessa vaguely. "Goodness, I haven't the faintest idea! I think you just suffer, or maybe you rub something on? Do you remember, Caroline?"

"Don't even remember your having it," said Caroline.

"I say, Caro," said Sara, "it's just as well we didn't find the proper department—they'd have thought I had smallpox or something—"

"I can't imagine *how* you'd have behaved if they had. Oh, Vanessa," giggled Caroline, "you should have *seen* Sara's face! And the way she bolted out of that door—" Caroline began to heave with silent laughter.

"But if you'd seen the faces of the patients in the ward I got into by mistake!" Sara began to giggle, too.

"Oh, Sara, you brute, you never told me about that," Caroline gasped, holding her tummy. "What happened? Did a nurse chase you?"

"Three!" hooted Sara, and collapsed on one of the beds. Caroline was rolling about on the other, and Vanessa looked at them, laughing a little and regretting that she seemed no longer to have the capacity for those painful, paralysing fits of giggling which used to attack her, too, when she was the age of Caroline and Sara.

There was a thunderous knock on the door, and John burst in.

"Will somebody," he demanded explosively, "*please* tell me what's happeing?" He looked coldly at the two gigglers on the bed. "First of all Sara and Caroline disappear. No sooner are they back than Sara and Vanessa vanish. Then Caroline goes, saying Sara has scarlet fever. And then about an hour later I find you, apparently all having hysterics."

"Oh, darling, I'm not!" said Vanessa.

"Oh, John, I haven't!" said Sara, sitting up and still giving a spasmodic giggle. "*Isn't* it a mercy?"

"John," said Caroline, wiping her eyes, "what did Vanessa use to cure her nettle-rash?"

"Nettle-rash?" queried John, out of his depth. "*I* don't know. Camo-something."

D

"Of course," said Vanessa, pleased: "Camomile. Or was it camembert? No, that's cheese, isn't it?"

"Gosh, I'm not putting cheese on myself—" said Sara.

"I haven't the least idea of what any of you are talking about, but I'm going to have the lot of you certified as soon as we get home," interrupted John severely. "If we ever do get home, which seems unlikely at the present rate of progress. Do you realise that I wanted to leave here at nine o'clock, and it's now three and a half minutes past eleven?"

"Goodness! So late!" said Vanessa, looking guilty. "I had no idea; oh, well, *now* we'd better look for a nice cheap place to have lunch, and then leave immediately after."

"No," said John, "I know you: we're leaving now. You people go and buy rolls and butter and anything else you fancy, within reason, and we shall picnic on the road."

"What road?" said Caroline. "Where do we go from here, John?"

"Well, I—er—" John rubbed the side of his nose and stammered a little. "I—er—haven't quite decided yet." He pulled a map out of his pocket and spread it on the bed, while the girls gathered round. "Here's Brussels," said John, pointing with a pencil. "And we can either go south to Rheims or"—he stopped and laughed a little and went on with a rush—"well, I thought that seeing we had already gone out of our way coming here we might as well go a bit farther, have a look at the Rhine and the Black Forest, make for Strasbourg and *then* Basle. What d'you say?"

"The Rhine!" said Sara. "Oh, John!"

"The Rhine!" said Vanessa. "How lovely— castles and the Lorelei and all that!"

"The Rhine!" said Caroline. "Have you a triptyque for Germany, and some Germany money? And have we time?"

"Oh, we've time enough!" answered John in marked contrast to his attitude of five minutes before. "And, just as it happens," he added, rubbing his nose again, "we have a triptyque, and I have some registered marks which we change at the first bank we see in Germany."

"John," accused Caroline, "you had all this planned. Me, I'd rather get to Switzerland right away, but—"

"Well, as a matter of fact, Caroline," interrupted John, "I'm rather like Sara—I feel that when we're within a few hundred miles of a place it seems a pity not to go and have a look at it. We might never be back on the Continent again," solemnly. "And *look* at these two, Caroline, just look at them. You couldn't disappoint them—"

"No," Caroline smiled, and made a horrible face at Sara, "no, we couldn't disappoint them."

CHAPTER FIVE

FOLLOWED a visit to the shops for rolls and butter and some cheese, and a lively ten minutes with a chemist, trying to bring home to him, by panto-mime and without actual demonstration ("For *none* of the places," Sara kept assuring Caroline in a worried voice, "are at *all* get-atable") the nature of her malady and her need for what she insisted on calling "calomine." He offered her cures for insect bites, rabies, scabies, while Caroline looked up her pocket dictionary and kept Sara informed as to what disease she was being suspected of next. Sara was becoming a little testy under these impu-tations, but just in time the chemist realized what they were after and handed over a bottle of pink lotion with smiling apologies for being so slow in the uptake.

"Scabies!" muttered Sara indignantly, climbing into Major Morris. "I say, Vanessa, what do I do with my medicine?"

"A tablespoonful three times a day after meals," Vanessa murmured.

Sara said, "Oh!" and wondered where she'd find a tablespoon, and thought with a little sigh that those odd picnic meals they were having didn't seem to come as often as three times a day.

"Vanessa, surely not!" exclaimed Caroline. "Surely camomile is put on, not inside you?"

"Oh, goodness, yes, how silly I am!" Vanessa

cried. "I was thinking of a tonic I had to take. Of course I remember now. When things get too unbearable, you dab on some lotion. Sara, darling, I might have poisoned you!"

"What a relief that would have been," said Caroline.

"Gosh—" Sara began, when John broke in:

"Is my hat there? Is—?"

"Is the luggage all right, is the cap on the petrol tank?" chanted Sara and Caroline in chorus, getting wise to him. "Yes. Yes. Yes."

So, with frequent stops, first for the apparently unending search for a *really* suitable spot for lunch, and then for Sara to get behind trees to anoint herself, they came finally, when it was becoming dusk, to Aachen and the German customs, where the great red and white posts, stretched across the road, barred their way.

Sara was thrilled, and was quite certain that any scene so romantic as this—the posts, with the car's headlights shining on them, the gathering dark, the man on guard, the little white office on the side of the road and its rather brusque official—couldn't fail to be the setting for something truly dramatic: for a string of stolen pearls to be hauled out by the official from the pocket of a fellow-traveller under their very eyes, or for the official to say suddenly, as he examined her passport, "Sara Storm, I arrest you as a spy," or for the whole party to be clapped into gaol, for Sara wasn't quite sure what reason. That now, would be life! But oddly enough nothing like that happened. The official cursorily inspected their bags and dismissed them; they strapped on their ungainly luggage and piled into the car; the white posts rose slowly—and they drove into Germany.

"Where are we making for, John?" asked Sara, as Vanessa took over the driving.

"Well," said John, "there's a little hotel a friend of mine told me about once—it's near a place called Konigswinter, which is south of Bonn. So if we can only find our way to Bonn, I believe we just keep along the Rhine until we reach this *Kurhaus*. It's at the foot of one of the *Sieben Gebirge.*"

"What are they?" Sara wanted to know, and John told her they were seven little hills along the Rhine, famous in song and story; and Sara asked why, and what were their names; and the insular Caroline said she'd be thankful to see a hill again; and Vanessa said that there was the rain, what a pity!"

"Oh, well," said Sara, "there's nothing to see now, anyway," so she took off her specs and snuggled up against Caroline for a little nap. It had been annoying Caroline slightly that what with her long legs and the bread-board and John's boots, she had not managed to snatch one wink of sleep in the car, while Sara, being little, had only to find a soft spot for her head somewhere on Caroline's anatomy and she would be asleep in half a second. Caroline liked the front seat better, and felt she could make herself very comfortable there; but she hadn't a hope of that, she thought regretfully, with John insisting that the back made him sick and Vanessa refusing to leave his side.

She had to at this point, however. John announced:

"I'm going to drive now. Vanessa, you hop into the back and have a rest—Caroline will take the torch and map-read for me."

It was a nerve-racking business, in the dark and the heavy, driving rain, finding their way in a strange country, even although Caroline was clever with maps and John had boundless confidence in his ability to reach any given spot; and it told on their tempers, too, for when Sara opened one eye and said sleepily: "There's something lacking. Definitely something lacking. Gosh, I know what it is—dinner! We've had no dinner, John. John, where do we stop for dinner?" John answered sourly, "do you see any likely-looking hostelry?"

"Gosh, *no!*" said Sara, peering, "I can't see anything."

"Neither can I," John replied, "so I should be obliged if you would keep quiet and allow me to concentrate on avoiding certain death in the ditch."

"Death in the Ditch," Sara, properly quelled, whispered to Vanessa: "that would make a lovely title for a thriller, wouldn't it? I say, Vanessa— *you* ask him about dinner."

"I wouldn't *dare,*" Vanessa whispered back. "But I think there was a roll left over from lunch if we could only find it." Then came various bumps and grunts from the back of the car as the search began.

Caroline's voice came from the front seat, clear and cold, "There are two rolls in a paper bag in the rack, if that's what you're looking for."

"Bother!" whispered Sara, fishing for them. "I was hoping they hadn't heard. Now we'll have to give them a bit."

"Caroline," shouted John, braking so abruptly that Vanessa swallowed a piece of dry roll in a hurry and nearly ended her career there and then, with Sara's thumps on her back to hasten her end. "Caroline, there's a signpost at last: I'll try and focus the spotlight and we'll see what it says."

Sara abandoned her kindly administrations on her cousin, and put on her specs to have a look, too.

"Bonn—twenty kilos," Caroline read, through the heavy rain. "And it's now," consulting the dash-board clock, "nine o'clock."

"Thank goodness Bonn is known around here," John said. "I thought we might be near Berlin by now."

"Oh, let's go to Berlin," came Sara's eager voice, "seeing we're near, anyway."

John began to make angry noises, and Vanessa begged Sara to say no more about going off their way again, for they seemed to have been doing too much of that; and in any case, in spite of what John had said, she was sure they were miles from Berlin. Sara vowed she'd never mention Berlin, Vienna, or Budapest again, and pointed out to Vanessa the adorable little black-and-white houses which appeared now and then as the headlights picked them up out of the darkness. Sweet, she thought they were. "That roll, or rather half-roll, helped," she went on, "but I still feel the pangs of hunger. Maybe if I had a wee sleep I wouldn't notice so much." So she composed herself against Vanessa and slept. John drove on.

Hunger, or the cessation of movement, woke Sara. "Gosh, are we there?" she said brightly. A dreadful silence, which even Sara noticed, greeted this remark. She pushed on her specs and looked out. The car was facing a fork in the road, the spot-light was illumining a signpost which said "Bonn—20k"; and the dashboard clock said eleven-fifteen.

"Gosh," said Sara, "we've been here before!"

John turned round in his seat and said savagely, "We've been here exactly five times before, you horrible child. We're haunted by this signpost—it follows us. Or else we're going round in circles—"

"Well, isn't that rather silly?" Sara was asking, piqued by the names John was calling her; when fortunately Vanessa's weary voice drowned hers, saying:

"Oh, John, darling, *couldn't* we sleep in the car?"

"No," said John firmly. "It would be ghastly. You get cold and stiff and sore. We'll have one more try."

And no one was more surprised than John when they found themselves, at midnight, crossing the Rhine at Bonn, and at one-thirty slipping quietly up to the Kurhaus Drachenfels where, by a miracle, lights still glowed.

"Gosh, that was *easy*!" Sara was heard to exclaim as they dismounted; and a delightful little smiling Boots assured them in excellent English they could have two rooms for the night, *and* some cold meat for their supper.

CHAPTER SIX

"WHAT really thrills me about this trip," Caroline woke next morning to hear Sara saying, "is arriving at places in the dark, with not the foggiest idea of what they look like, and then discovering them in the morning. Come on, Caro; do get up, and we'll explore."

"I don't feel in the least ready to get up," Caroline complained, "for I spent half the night fishing these crazy bedclothes off the floor. Did ever you see anything so silly?" She lay looking gloomily at the enormous bolster-cum-eiderdown, buttoned into a spotless white linen slip, which was all the beds had in place of the accustomed blankets and sheets.

"I thought they were jolly comfortable," said Sara, who enjoyed above all things (except perhaps really good thrillers) habits and customs different from those at home: "so cosy—like sleeping between two feather beds. Fancy, nobody ever told me that German beds were different from ours."

"If any one had told me I should have stayed at home," Caroline answered. "I finally had to anchor the miserable thing on to the bed with my coat."

"Well, don't brood on it," said Sara, who was one of those awkward people who seem to enjoy getting-up for getting-up's sake and who remain consistently cheerful on it. "I've anointed myself *all* over and I think I've cowed that foul nettle-rash —I don't look nearly so diseased this morning. And now I do want to explore, so *get up*; or I'll remove your big bolster."

Caroline crawled out of bed. "Oh, do go away and climb the Seven Mountains and leave me in peace!" she growled.

Sara thought that wasn't at all a bad idea, but that *seven* hills was just overdoing it a bit, and that she would wait for Caroline and then they could climb the Drachenfels—at whose foot the Kurhaus lay. Caroline hadn't the faintest intention of going near the Drachenfels at that uncivilized hour, but she consented to have a look round the village, which was called Rhondorf and was quite enchanting, with little white houses, black-beamed, and a little round church stuck in the middle. The main road passed by the Kurhaus while small, twisted streets straggled off it towards the Drachenfels which rose behind, tree-covered, a miniature mountain. The bad weather had spent itself in the night, and the sun was shining on the roofs and the streets, still wet.

"Oh, gosh, Caro!" Poor Sara was almost speechless with delight. "Isn't it thrilling? And can you believe that we're actually on the banks of the *Rhine*?"

"It's difficult," said Caroline, "for I can see no sign of it. I suppose it's somewhere beyond the road. We might go and look for it, if you like."

"I'd love it, but I'm kind of peckish now—let's look for Van and John and breakfast instead."

They found all three in the Kurhaus dining-room, the first two looking exceedingly low in their spirits. Sara smiled on the Boots, who had turned into a waiter, and sat down.

"Oh, hallo, you two! "she rattled. "Isn't this the most marvellous village? Caro and I have been *all* over it—pass me a roll, please, Vanessa; *and* the honey, John, please—we're going to have a look at the Rhine after breakfast, and did you have queer feather-beds instead of blankets? Old Caroline didn't sleep a wink. Oh, and my nettle-rash is much better, you'll be glad to hear."

"What a pity," murmured Vanessa, stirring her coffee moodily. Sara looked surprised at this unusual lack of sympathy, but before she could get her mouth emptied sufficiently to protest, Caroline said:

"Of course I slept. What's the matter with you pair? Quarrelled?"

"We've no money," said John.

"You never do have, do you?" Caroline was unperturbed.

"No, but I mean it literally, this time."

"But John," said Caroline accusingly, "you *said* you had registered marks or something—"

"So we have. But, I must explain, as it seems to have escaped your notice, that this is Sunday—registered marks are kind of travellers' cheques which you change into money, and there are no banks open to change them."

"Gosh!" said Sara. "What do we do? Cut and run? Pass me some more bread, *quick.*"

"Unprincipled little glutton," John said.

"But, John," said Caroline, "what *do* we do? Can't the hotel change you some English money? I'm sure that nice waiter would do anything for us."

"Yes, we could, but the rate of exchange is so bad in that case—only twelve marks to the pound instead of the twenty we get with registered marks. We can't afford to lose eight bob on every pound. No, we'll just have to wait here until to-morrow, when the banks open."

"But that's simply super," exulted Sara. "It's a pet of a place. Cheer up, you owls, you'll love it."

"*Can* we stay here?" Caroline asked. "Can the hotel give us rooms?"

"We'll ask our waiter," said John, "but for the love of goodness don't give the show away in case he turns us out."

The little waiter, who seemed to be the mainstay and prop of the establishment, had the question put to him. To his great regret, he replied, a large party was expected that afternoon, and not a room in the hotel would be free. But, he went on, perhaps relenting at the look of dismay on at least three of the faces before him, there was a house nearby which let rooms. No doubt it could be arranged that they sleep there, and have their meals in the hotel.

This was generally agreed to be better and better; John and Vanessa cheered up, and, as soon as Sara's enormous appetite was satisfied, they moved off to inspect their new quarters in a clean little house in a winding street behind the Kurhaus. Rather to Sara's regret, it wasn't black-and-white, but it had bright geraniums in window-boxes to make up. Inside they found luxurious bedrooms with running water, smart little bedside lamps and electric switches on the walls which, to Sara's amusement, went round and round instead of up and down.

"Isn't this *nice*?" said Caroline, bouncing on one bed, while Vanessa, with some vague sense of a housewife's duties, thumped the other one with her fist, and no very clear idea of what to demand from a bed.

John poked his smiling face round the door just then, having returned from looking over the other room.

"Oh, John," Vanessa called out, "this is palatial—but won't it simply ruin us?"

John's grin broadened. "All this luxury," he announced, "is ours for the modest sum of one mark fifty per room, per night—which, being interpreted, is about one and sixpence! Now come on, and let's have a look at Rhondorf."

They collected themselves and wandered down to the river's edge, and Sara kept saying that she'd love to go on one of the little river steamers and wasn't it a pity they had no money? And Caroline finally said that if Sara didn't stop nagging about going on the river, she wouldn't have any further use for money, and Sara wanted to know why not, and Caroline told her in a sinister voice to wait and she'd see.

"Oh, rubbish!" said Sara. "Now look—if you all stand out on that breakwater, I'll take your photograph. And I must have the river in."

John and Caroline, knowing Sara's way with a camera, groaned, but Vanessa said in her kind voice, "That will be nice, Sara dear," and went and posed herself as gracefully as a rather slippery breakwater would let her, with the great river flowing behind her, followed by the grumbling Caroline and John. Sara arranged them and rearranged them, and Caroline remarked that if Sara didn't take more care she'd be in the river, hopping about like that, but finally Sara had them placed to her satisfaction.

"Now all say 'lilies'—it gives a nice expression," she commanded, peering into her viewfinder. "Oh, blow—the sun's in the wrong place!" The group stopped saying "lilies" and relaxed.

"I'm sure the sun won't mind moving round for you," said Caroline.

"It's quite all right," Sara assured her: "it'll do just as well if you all come and stand where I am, and I'll go down to the end and face the other way." So with admirable patience the group formed again, facing the river, while Sara backed down the breakwater, head bent over her camera. "Come down a bit, will you?" she said. "I want more river."

She got it. Eager for a really worthy picture, she took a sudden step to the right, skidded on the slimy stones, and, with a cry, splashed backwards into the Rhine.

The others leapt forward, but too late to save her. "Oh, dear," moaned Vanessa, "she'll be drowned! She'll be carried downstream and drowned!"

"Not she," said John; "the breakwater'll stop her." Caroline said nothing, but dropped on her knees and thrust her face down to the water—just in time to meet Sara's coming up.

"Ow!" she said. "Do look where you're going, Sara!" Sara, choking and half-blinded, and thinking it wasn't going to be much fun if Caroline intended to clout her on the head every time she came to the surface, scrabbled at the slippery break-water with one hand and stretched out the other to clutch something more substantial. It happened to be Caroline's arm—and it proved but a broken reed. Taken by surprise, the weight of Sara plus Rhine water was too much for Caroline; she lost her balance, and with an infuriated shout of "Look *out,* you idiot! John! Help!" was dragged into the river. And the really reprehensible bit about it all was that John was laughing too much to be a help to any one. But Vanessa's righteous anger, and the sight of the two bedraggled speci-mens clinging side by side to the breakwater, sobered him up, so he lay flat on his face on the stones, grumbling about the effect on his good flannel trousers, while Vanessa sat on his legs lest he should disappear too, and he stretched out a strong left arm to Caroline first, then to Sara.

"Rescue of the Rhine-maidens," he commented;

"but I've never seen a Rhine-maiden with specs before—although it's a miracle you didn't lose them down there in the mud, Sara."

"I've lost my camera," Sara mourned, scrubbing her curls vigorously with Vanessa's pocket-handkerchief.

"I'd shut up about cameras and photography if I were you," whispered John, glancing at Caroline, who was wringing out her skirt as best she could, with an expression of utter loathing on her face. "But never mind, infant—I'll buy you a camera as soon as I have some money again."

"Now I think you should both hurry back to the Kurhaus, have hot baths, and go to bed," counselled Vanessa, who when she did remember her responsibilities did it in style.

After getting rid of Rhine water and an enormous lunch, at which the little Boots tended them like a mother (his only unfortunate remark being, as he glanced at the girls' wet hair, "So! You bathe very early!"), Caroline's faith in human nature was somewhat restored, and she consented to join Sara in the garden with a book, to let the sun dry their hair. It was a pleasant garden, with a grand view of the Drachenfels, but Sara lay flat on her stomach and buried her little tip-tilted nose in *Tales of Mystery* and spared the surroundings never a glance. Caroline desultorily turned over the pages of a guide book (which John had had concealed in the car) and kept reading little bits out to Sara, who paid her no attention at all. Vanessa

E

and John were having a quiet doze in camp-chairs a little way off.

After about an hour, Caroline felt an unaccustomed urge for action. She slammed shut her guide and announced, "I'm going to climb the Dragon's Rock and look for the cave where Siegfried slew the dragon. There's another story I like better, about the old dragon swallowing a ship loaded with gunpowder; and the fire that dragons have in their tummies exploded it and blew the old chap to bits. Serve him right for a greedy beast. Nearly as greedy as you, Sara, you fat and lazy creature." Sara grunted but said nothing. Caroline went over and roused the others, who thought, yes, decidedly they must go up the Drachenfels. Only after some uncommonly sharp prods with Caroline's toe in the direction of Sara's ribs did that connoisseur in thrills take time to reply:

"Shut up, Caroline, this is colossal. Listen: *'Inch by inch—line by line—with a descent only appreciable at intervals that seemed ages—down and still down it came! Days passed—it might have been that many days had passed—ere it swept so closely over me as to fan me with its acrid breath. The odour of the sharp steel forced itself into my nostrils. I prayed—I wearied heaven with my prayer for its more speedy descent. I grew frantically mad, and struggled to force myself upward against the sweep of the fearful scimitar.'"* She sighed deeply. "Isn't that terrific?"

"Gigantic, stupendous. Bring it with you—we're going up the Drachenfels. Have you walking-shoes on?" Sara mumbled a yes, and rose and followed the others, still reading. The path wound round the little hill, deep among the trees, and Caroline told Sara that she ought to find climbing up the Drachenfels, on the banks of the Rhine, much more exciting than silly old thrills.

It came as a great shock to all of them, used as they were to lonely Scottish hills, to find a flourishing open-air restaurant at the top, with a band playing for all it was worth, while fat, jolly Germans drank beer and enjoyed their Sunday afternoon enormously. Sara immediately went off and sat at a remote and tenantless table and got down to *Tales of Mystery* again. The other three gazed rather pathetically at the happy throng, and Vanessa made swallowing noises in her dry throat and said, "A long, cool drink would have been rather nice, wouldn't it?"

"Hush, woman!" said her husband. "Did no one ever tell you that the best things in life are free? Let us enjoy the sunshine, and go and look at the view. Get Sara, Caroline."

But Sara felt no urge to look at the view. "I never thought much of views," she informed Caroline. "I never could understand why people take so much trouble to get them. Go away." Caroline went.

When, some five minutes later, Sara looked up with a grunt of impatience at the interruption, and saw a tall, white-aproned figure patiently waiting for her order, she said automatically, "Lemonade, please."

The waiter, who was learning English in his spare

time, was delighted at being able to understand, and Sara had scarcely reached the next paragraph when he was back with her drink, beaming.

"Danke schön," said Sara, and it was practically all the German she knew.

"Thank *you,"* the waiter answered, and went off —rather reluctantly—to serve another customer.

"This was a good idea," thought Sara, knocking back her lemonade. "Gosh, I was thirsty!" Halfway through she put down her glass suddenly and felt sick. "I've no money," she thought. "Caroline's got no money. John's got no money. Vanessa never has any money. *Nobody's* got any money. Oh, gosh, what'll I do? I can't return it now. Here I am sitting in a strange café on the top of a mountain" (Sara was getting a little excited) "drinking lemonade, and I've no money. I'll just have to run for it." This wasn't striking her as the good idea it had seemed when talking to John that morning. "Oh, gosh, they'll see me! I'll have to use stealth." She looked over towards her waiter, a subtle casual glance, she felt, but which in reality more resembled the look a defenceless big-game hunter might cast at an approaching man-eating tiger. But the tiger fortunately, was being kept busy at other tables. "I'll do it in stages," thought Sara. "First I'll nip under the table, then, when the coast's clear, make a quick crawl behind that tree. What a *mercy* there's no one at this end of the café!" A hasty reconnoitre, and then she ducked down. She got under the table all right, although she did feel it was a pity that one of the little iron chairs was knocked over in the process; but what she had not realised was that a bare iron-topped table did not provide the maximum of cover. She sat on the grass, however, and hugged her knees, thinking how queer human legs and table legs looked from that angle, when a horribly familiar pair of legs in a white apron hove in view, and her waiter's solemn face came down to within an inch of her own, and her waiter's voice spoke a great spatter of German which sounded very fierce.

"Ich verstehe nicht," said Sara. Neither did she, but she put on a particularly stupid expression, thinking that if she pretended to be a bit off in the top she might get away with it yet. However, the waiter beamed, and in a very slow and laborious way said:

"You haf lost nothing."

"No," Sara agreed, crawling out rather shamefacedly, "I have lost nothing." She sat down again beside her lemonade and decided to try a spot of flattery. "You speak English so well," she said, slowly and a little loudly, for she always had it fixed in her mind that foreigners were deaf. The waiter looked coy, and wrapped one leg round the other. Sara decided to take the plunge and confess all.

"Herr Ober," she said, in her politest voice, "I am afraid I have no money."

Herr Ober grinned, for naturally he knew that the English *always* had money. And it was some little time before Sara managed to convince him that the impossible had happened and that she really had no money; and the telling took a lot of patience; and constant reference to her English-

German Conversational Dictionary, not to mention *All you want to know in Germany,* which didn't really provide for the present contingency; and a more or less complete resume of the whole tour. Herr Ober was enormously interested and felt he was learning a lot of new words, but at the end of it had no more idea what to do than Sara, for there was the lemonade, ordered and half-finished—and there was Sara, without a *pfennig.*

Suddenly his eye became fixed on Sara's handsome copy of *Tales of Mystery and Imagination* towards which he had been casting envious looks throughout the conversation.

"That is an English book?" he asked. Sara nodded abstractedly, and thought, "Gosh, what a silly man he is! Fancy starting about books in the middle of a crisis like this!" But Herr Ober wasn't so silly, as was evident when he propounded his scheme to Sara. It appeared that his great desire, and his great difficulty, was the obtaining of English books to further his studies, and he now suggested that if Sara gave him her so-wonderfully beautiful book he would himself pay for her lemonade.

"Oh, gosh, I can't do that!" said Sara: "I'm reading it. Besides, it's not my book." Herr Ober pointed out that the lemonade, of which Sara had made so free, wasn't his lemonade, and that surely it was a small price to pay to avoid a dreadful fate, unspecified. Sara, thoroughly alarmed, gave in, but insisted on having his name and address and a promise that whenever she sent him sufficient money to buy another English book, he would send on to her *Tales of Mystery.* "You won't like it, anyway," she told him, "it's not your style at all."

But Herr Ober just smiled at her, and stroked his new possession, and Sara rather gloomily thought she'd better go and find the others before they found *her* and had to be told of her misdeeds. So she hurried away, but hurried back to finish her lemonade, which she felt was indeed hers now that she had paid for it so dear.

How dear, she fortunately had no means of knowing.

CHAPTER SEVEN

MONDAY morning saw the party's coffers filled, their bills duly paid, and, after a reluctant farewell to Rhondorf, steady progress being made up the Rhine. Caroline felt, and said, that she was frankly disappointed with the Rhine.

"*I* think," said Sara, "that the Rhine's superb. It grows on you, Caroline darling," she went on airily, "and that queer yellowy-greeny-grey colouring reminds me of a picture by Cezanne." At this unusual evidence of culture Caroline was struck dumb, and John was so astounded that he turned his head to see if Sara still looked her normal self, and in so doing failed to notice that the road turned off while the little railway line, that was keeping the road company, went on, and drove Major Morris on to the permanent way with a most sickening lurch.

The Major was apparently unharmed, and John, on the road again, hurried on, suddenly showing a great desire to make speed. He did sanction a stop at Koblenz, and led them, on the run, up to the fortress of Ehrenbreitstein, allowed them one look at the Mosel joining the Rhine, then ran them down again.

Even Caroline enthused at the scenery from Koblenz to Bingen, and though Sara missed the Lorelei rock, through having a little nap, John took care to point out the Mouse Tower where, he said, the wicked Bishop Hatto was devoured by mice for his sins; for Sara's horror of mice was always giving rise to little touches like that from the more hard-hearted members of her family.

"There's one thing," said Sara, trying to forget the Bishop and his awful fate, "to be thankful for —we don't do much actual sight-seeing on this trip."

"Gracious me, no!" said John: "you're seeing the country."

They left the Rhine at Bingen, to their great sorrow, and missed the river very much until, late in the afternoon, they cheered up at the sight of Heidelberg and the Neckar. There they had a large and early dinner and immediately after John ordered them off again with Vanessa at the wheel.

"After dawdling along for days," murmured Caroline, "John suddenly decides he's in a hurry."

"Insubordinate imp," said John. "No, but I have just realised that my conference has its first session on Thursday morning, which means being in Basle Wednesday evening, and I want to have a quick look at the Black Forest."

"Plenty of time, I should think," said Caroline, studying the map.

At eight o'clock Vanessa said, "Don't you think we might find some place to stop the night, darling?"

"No, no," said John, "we must go on."

At nine o'clock, Vanessa said, "Don't you think we might——"

"No, no," said John, "on a bit yet."

At ten o'clock, Vanessa said, "Don't you think——?"

"No, no," said John, "we must push on."

"Don't be brutal, John," said Caroline; "we'll not get in anywhere if we wait much longer, and Sara has been asleep for hours, the lucky thing. Where are you aiming for, anyway?"

"Baden-Baden," said John. "We're nearly there."

"Oh, but darling, that's a terribly grand sort of spa-spa!" said Vanessa, who was tired. "We'll never get bed and breakfast for one and sixpence there."

"All right." Economy could move John where human sympathy failed signally. "We'll stop at the first decent-looking *gasthaus* we see."

"Too dark to see if it looks decent," Caroline pointed out, but half-heartedly, since she was too weary to care.

"Here's a village——" said Vanessa.

"And here's a *gasthaus*," said John, pulling up at the Gasthof zur Krone. They left Sara sleeping in the car while they entered to investigate. They found a low-ceiled *gaststube* with tables and chairs, empty but for a young girl, rather shy, rather pretty, who said in reply to John that there were certainly two rooms which they could have. To inspect, the party trooped upstairs, and found a most overwhelming apartment, all pink and white and gold, with fat cherubs painted on the ceiling. They gazed, awestruck.

"My dears," said Vanessa, "this is positively bridal! Or d'you think it's the royal suite? I certainly must spend at least one night in this gorgeousness." The other two daren't trust themselves to reply, so John in a strangled kind of voice asked about the other room. Their young hostess, well pleased with the effect of the cherubs, led them downstairs again, through the *gaststube* into a large, clean, airy enough room with two neat little beds, whose only peculiarity was, on one of them, a huge basket of eggs, which was nonchalantly removed.

"This is all right," said Caroline, "but what's that funny, bumping noise? Ask her, John, will you please?"

John asked, and at the girl's reply turned with an unnaturally solemn face to Caroline and said, "Your fellow-guests, Caroline. The cows. The byre is just through there," and he waved his arm towards a door in the left-hand wall.

"Christmas!" Caroline said. "We do see life. Better not tell Sara: she'd have ten thousand fits."

John, his duty done as the only German speaker in the party, went out to collect the somnolent Sara and to put the car away, while Vanessa drifted back into the common room with Caroline at her heels.

"Caroline darling," she said, "I'm *filthy*. D'you think you could very cleverly extract some hot water from the little wench—"

"Hot water?" interrupted Sara coming in, rather bleary and still half-asleep. "I could enjoy a bath. Is there a bath?"

Caroline thought of the proximity of the cow-house and said she doubted it.

It must have been somewhere round about the small hours when Sara, for all the exquisite comfort of her bed, found herself wide awake, listening.

"There's a jolly queer noise in this room," she thought: "sounds like heavy breathing or something. Maybe old Caroline had developed adenoids in the night."

The heavy breathing became worse and developed more into a snuffling.

"Gosh!" thought Sara: "I don't think adenoids could make all that noise. Besides, Caroline hasn't got any—she had 'em hacked out years ago. *Gosh*, she must be choking—I'd better wake her!" She leant over to the other bed, near enough to hear Caroline's faint, regular breathing, and to realise that it certainly wasn't Caroline who was puffing and blowing. "Oh, gosh," shrinking back under her feather bed, "we're being robbed and murdered in our beds! Or maybe," and her terror, if anything, increased, "or maybe it's a ghost." She lay and trembled; far from thinking "Ah!—adventure at last!" which one might have expected; she lay, wishing that she was hundreds of miles away in her adventureless little bed at home, that she had never come for this ghastly holiday, that Caroline would waken. "Gosh, what'll I do? If I waken Caro, it will hear me. But I can't stand it—I'm going to scream—oh, gosh! *What's that?*"

That was a series of muffled thumps from the intruder which at least had the desired effect of wakening Caroline, who turned over and muttered sleepily:

"Do shut up, Sara!"

"It's not me," Sara hissed indignantly, "wake up, Caroline, there's something in the room!"

"Don't be silly," said Caroline's muffled voice.

"Oh, Caroline, *do* wake up! Listen! *Now,* can't you hear It?" What with the bumps and thumps and snuffles Caroline, even half-asleep as she was, would have been deaf indeed if she hadn't. She sat up.

"What on *earth* is it?" she whispered.

"It's a horrible great man going to steal our money and probably murder us," Sara quavered.

"Well, he's making a lot of noise about it," Caroline answered, as the sounds continued.

"Yes." Sara's voice got smaller and smaller. "I was afraid so. It's a monster."

"Oh, what rot!" said Caroline, very, very briskly, but still quietly. "Get up, Sara, and put on the light."

"Get up?" in a shrill crescendo. "I'd rather die."

"Maybe you will, if you stay where you are,"

said Caroline ghoulishly. But realising that this time Sara was not to be bullied, she sighed and added, "Oh, well! I'll have to get up myself."

"Oh, don't, *don't!*" moaned Sara. "Don't, Caroline." But by this time the visitor—man or spirit-sounded as if it were trying to batter the walls down, fortunately, however, at the other end of the room from the light switch, so Caroline sidled cautiously out of bed and round the wall to the door. She snapped on the light, and this time Sara did scream, and then dived under the feather bed-not *nearly* so comforting, either, as a good pile of blankets. For there, beyond Caroline's bed, by the chair, was the most fearsome apparition, with four legs and a hairy body and a head which was a great white crumpled—*nothing.*

For a few minutes Sara was deaf to Caroline's injunctions to come to the surface; but when she realised that it was laughter and not the death-rattle which was choking Caroline's voice, she did look out with one cautious eye. Caroline was sitting at the foot of Sara's bed, giggling and holding out Sara's glasses to her.

"Put 'em on," she said, "and have a look." Sara obeyed meekly enough, and then gave a crow of laughter—rather wobbly, but authentic.

"Caroline, it's a darling! But how did a calf get in here? And what's that over its head? Gosh, *my clean blouse* which I laid ready for the morning, the little brute!" Sara was quick enough getting out of bed to rescue her property, although she did try to insist that it was to save the poor little calf from blundering into any more furniture. "But how did

it get *in*? That's what I can't understand," she said.

"Well," Caroline replied, "it's really not surprising when you think that we share a communicating door with the cowshed."

"What?" gasped Sara.

"Oh, yes," Caroline assured her nonchalantly, "that door, now half-open, leads, as you might guess from the perfume being wafted from it, to the byre."

"Well, for the love of Allah, let's get it shut, or we'll have the whole herd in!" Sara was fond of cows, in their place, but she had clear views that their place wasn't her bedroom.

"I shouldn't think so," Caroline was comforting. "They'll all be tied up. This wee chap must have got loose and somehow pushed the bolt back. Or maybe he was so young they didn't bother to tie him up. We had better send him home." But would the wee chap go? He had had his taste of freedom and luxury, and he wasn't going back to a smelly old stall for any one. Sara and Caroline cajoled and urged and threatened, but through that door he would not move. He floundered on to Sara's bed, accompanied by a scream of rage from her; he knocked over a chair piled with their clothes, and put his foot in the bucket of water provided for their ablutions, while the two pursued him, at first gently, but gradually becoming noisier and wilder until the place was pandemonium.

"Obstinate?" panted Caroline as they paused to draw breath, and the calf regarded them innocently from a strategic point by the window and began to

lick the wall. "Let's give up the struggle and go back to bed. Maybe he'll lie down then, or return to his cow-house."

"Yes, but maybe he'll lie down on the top of me," Sara demurred; "or he'll forget to shut that door, and we'll be over-run with cows."

"Not to mention the odour," agreed Caroline.

"What I'd like to know is why the innkeeper and his daughter aren't wakened by all this row and come and look after their silly animals," Sara said crossly.

"Oh, I expect they're so used to this sort of thing, they just sleep through it," answered Caroline. "Come on, Sara, both together—when I say three, jump for his neck and we'll *drag* him through."

And there they both were, one pushing, the other clinging round the calf's neck and pulling, when the innkeeper's daughter—and the innkeeper—found them. And, as Sara pointed out when it was all over, and they were able to contemplate spending the remainder of the night in peace, it was a bit thick, after all they had been through, to be accused of trying to *steal* the animal.

CHAPTER EIGHT

"This is nice," said Sara next morning, as they drove through a lovely, undulating, wooded landscape, John's hat, the luggage, and the cap on the petrol tank all safe, "but I wish we could come to the Black Forest."

"This is the Black Forest," said John.

"But it's not black," Sara wailed.

"It's not even a forest," sniffed Caroline.

Vanessa murmured something about ungrateful little horrors, while John said:

"I suppose you two wanted to hack your way through impenetrable forest with an axe in one hand and a lantern in the other? But actually I believe the depths are truly black. Here we're on the fringes—"

"And it's rather fun really, now that I know it *is* the Black Forest," Caroline was becoming enthusiastic.

"I *wish* it were winter," Sara sighed, "and I'd ski along the *skiwegs,* chasing bandits. Can we get out and explore, John?"

John was apparently inclined to be more lenient that morning. They stopped at Hundseck and had coffee and a stroll round the swimming-pool and along one of the little paths.

Then they came to the Mummelsee, lying still and quiet in the sun, encircled by trees. "The Mummelsee is the home of the *Mummelweibchen,*"

Caroline told them, in a dramatic voice: "water-sprites who are water-lilies by day and maidens by night; they are very, very beautiful—but whoever goes near them is never seen again."

"Well!" said Sara and Vanessa, impressed.

"I dare say," said John, "but now I'll tell *you* something. That hill you see there is the Hornis-grinde, is four thousand feet high—*and* you're all going to the top and down again before you have any lunch." Caroline groaned, but up they all went, and even Sara declared it was worth coming up to see to the west the great flat plain of the Rhine with France beyond, while to the south lay, in complete contrast, the hills and trees of the Schwarz-wald.

And, as they had hoped, but no one really expected, they were in Basle that evening.

"I think," said John at dinner, "that instead of you people wasting your time here for a couple of days, you ought to go on to Grindelwald by train, and I'll follow as soon as I can. I've already booked rooms at the Hotel Alpenrose—I've no idea *what* it's like, Sara—and I'll send a telegram to say you'll arrive to-morrow. There's a nice train leaves for Interlaken about seven-fifty."

"Oh help!" said Caroline. "It couldn't be a nice train if it leaves at seven-fifty. But it's a good idea all the same," she continued later to Sara. "It'll be a relief to see some mountains—only, I'm amazed at Vanessa consenting to abandon her husband."

"I wish John could have been persuaded to let

F

us have the car," said Sara. "And I hope old Van doesn't fuss us to death when she has to look after us all by herself."

But fuss or no fuss, seven-fifty next morning saw the three of them safely in the Interlaken train, and Caroline's book on Germany, whence she had secretly derived her amazing knowledge, was replaced by one on Switzerland.

"It says here," said Caroline, coming out into the open this time and reading aloud, "that Swiss trains are so clean that you can open a bar of Swiss chocolate, lay it on the window sill of your train, pick it up half an hour hence, and eat it without a quiver!"

"That's all very well," said Sara, "but I could never leave chocolate half an hour, could you? What does it say about Switzerland being a complete wash-out?" she grumbled on. *"I thought Switzerland was all lovely mountains, and the whole of it so far is as flat as a pancake."*

"Sara, darling," Vanessa soothed, "you're so all-or-nothing, so impatient. Just wait."

And sure enough, when they had passed through Berne, the mountains began to glow in the distance, and Sara and Caroline and Vanessa began to get more and more excited. Sara especially could hardly contain herself, and when the train ran along between the mountains on the one hand and Lake Thun on the other, she very nearly had a stroke, running from one side of the train to the other, lest she should miss *anything,* and kept pointing out the little red-roofed villages on the lake, and once two swans so near that she felt she could lean out of the train and touch them.

"There it is! There it is!" some of the other passengers along the corridor set up a cry.

"There's *what*? What *is* it?" Sara asked, hurling herself away from the lake-side windows.

"*I* dunno," said Caroline; then, overhearing, she added carelessly, "It's the Jungfrau or something, apparently," but when they had their first glimpse of the Jungfrau's remote loveliness they decided it was worth becoming worked-up about.

The meadows were decked with flowers, and the fruit trees were in blossom as they left Interlaken. "I knew it," said Sara with satisfaction: "we're *not* too early for the flowers, although every one at home said May was a silly time to come to Switzerland." Caroline thought that Grindelwald, being higher, would be more backward in the way of flowers; Vanessa, in a dream, ventured no opinion. Sara was jumping about like a cricket, one minute looking out at the flowers, the next gazing fascinated at the peaked cap of the guard who had come to have a look at their tickets.

They all felt, when they reached Grindelwald, that it was a pity that John hadn't been more explicit about the hotel he had booked, for only after—to Caroline's distress—making a scene at the Alpenrose where they were obviously neither expected nor welcomed, and rousing the entire station and its environs, did they discover that there was another Hotel Alpenrose at a village a little farther down the valley, and that although the train didn't descend again until two-fifteen, the station-master had a friend who would be more than willing to drive them back in his automobile.

Sara was furious, for the Grindelwald Alpenrose was quite impressive with bright green shutters and gay window-boxes; and the other Alpenrose, which they reached in about five minutes, wasn't a hotel at all, she declared, only a chalet. Caroline and Vanessa reserved judgment, for it was rather sweet, brown and green and white, with an apple-tree in bloom at the side; but it was certainly very small and modest, and the proprietor himself carried in their bags, and their rooms hadn't even any wall-paper, as Sara took care to point out, just the bare pine boards; but it was scrupulously clean and fresh, even to the crisp white lace curtains that hung over the windows.

"We can always move back to the other Alpen-rose," Vanessa tried to placate Sara as they con-ferred, after Vanessa had murmured something to the innkeeper about baths, then lunch, "if we don't like it after to-night." Caroline thought of the young innkeeper's pleased look of welcome as he carried in their bags, and wondered miserably how they were going to break it to him that they didn't like his little hotel, but all she said was:

"It's perhaps nicer being out of Grindelwald, and we're certainly nearer the mountains."

"So near," snapped Sara, "that you'll have to lie on your back if you want to see the top of that monstrous great thing over there. And we'll have to walk miles before we even *see* a shop or can do a thing."

Baths, and an enormous lunch, improved their

tempers wonderfully. They ate in a bright little dining-room which, appropriately enough, had a pot of Alpine roses on the window-sill, and to Sara's intense joy, a little bowl of real, live gentians on the table. A small maiden of about sixteen, with a round face and not a word of English or French, waited on them, and when they had finished, the innkeeper, who spoke fluent English and whose name was Fritz Berger, came in to see that they were being properly fed. Caroline took him outside and got him to name the mountains—the Eiger opposite, then the Mettenberg, and up at the head of the valley, a frame for Grindelwald, the Wetterhorn. He told her there was a hill path to Grindelwald behind the inn, and from up there could be seen many more mountains—the Finsteraarhorn, and the Schreckhorn, the Monch, and the Jungfrau herself. Caroline thought that they ought to set off to see them all at once, but for some unaccountable reason Vanessa insisted on writing to John. "And you two ought to write to the parents to say we've arrived safely," she said.

"I don't suppose they'll be interested, since they're tripping about Norway, but we'll buy a post-card in the village," said Caroline. "And must you write now, Van? He'll be here before a letter will reach him."

"Better send him a telegram," Sara suggested, and Vanessa, to their surprise, was content with this idea.

The hill path did not materialise. There were so many paths, and so many chalets to confuse them, and the path they did choose brought them down almost immediately on to the road again. So they continued by the road, determining to find the the path later.

Grindelwald was a friendly little place, and it was some consolation to Sara to discover that nearly all the grand hotels were closed, "so we couldn't have stayed there anyway," she thought. They found exquisite post-cards—photographs and, for Sara, coloured flower pictures; and the shopkeepers in the main street had laid out trestle-tables, covered, simply covered with carved wood in seemingly endless shapes and varieties; and only the finding of a cafe, where they sat outside in the sunshine and had cakes and hot chocolate, dragged Sara away from the array. And then, oddly, it appeared to be time to go back and have dinner, which was another huge meal. And by the time nine o'clock came they found, to their intense surprise, they really couldn't keep their eyes open another minute, and all three of them went off to bed.

"This is a sweet little room," said Sara, lying in bed, gazing short-sightedly at a highly-coloured representation of the Falls of the Rhine on the wall opposite as she waited for Caroline to cope with shutters and the light and get into the other bed.

"Yes," said Caroline, without a tremor. "I like the plain walls, too, don't you?"

CHAPTER NINE

WHEN Vanessa came downstairs next morning she found the two sitting in the sun at a little round table under the apple tree, poring over *Walks and Excursions in the Valley of Grindelwald,* which they had bought the day before in the village, while Sara absently fondled the Alpenrose dog which lay drowsing at her feet. She looked up as Vanessa approached.

"Oh, it's you!" she said. "I thought it was breakfast. Good morning. Isn't it a marvellous day? And Vanessa, there are *two* glaciers near Grindelwald, isn't it thrilling? And did you notice that even the bathroom has gorgeous views of the mountains? Shall we go there now?"

"Let's have breakfast first," suggested Caroline, as it was borne unsteadily out by the little maid. While they ate, they argued.

"Glaciers," insisted Sara. "First the Lower, then the Upper."

"I think," said Caroline, "we should climb the hill behind the Alpenrose. There are two chalets up there, just perched on nothing—look, you can see them if you come over here—with trees and a little bit of green round them. I'd like to go there." Sara put on her glasses and looked up-about two miles, she felt—up the hillside where Caroline pointed.

"I'm going to write letters," said Vanessa

"and if you took my advice you would both be better having a quiet morning round about here."

Sara and Caroline looked at each other and grinned.

After breakfast the two of them quietly made off by the path behind Alpenrose. They walked up beside the little stream that brawled noisily down the hill, *Walks and Excursions* in Caroline's pocket.

"Gosh, it's steep!" puffed Sara. "Gosh, *Caroline,* just look at the flowers on that bank!"

"Nothing but dandelions," said Caroline annoyingly. "I don't think much of that. Plenty of them at home."

"Caro, how can you—there are thousands of things there—violets and forget-me-nots and those yellow things, globe-flowers are they called? And another yellow one, and orchis—and oh, gosh, *funny* wee gentians, not like the ones in the dining-room! I must get a book about them all."

"Meantime," Caroline said, though she secretly thought the flowers were perfect, "if you'd take your nose out of that bank we might get somewhere before lunch."

"Where are we going?" Sara asked.

"Oh, just up!" replied Caroline. "I would like to reach those chalets, and there's a waterfall called Abbach mentioned in the book—we might find that."

They went up and up, and the brook turned and twisted and fell in the most delicious little waterfalls, and always, whenever they stopped and looked round, there were the mountains above them —the Jungfrau slipped into view, and others whose names they didn't know—and at their feet the flowers. When Sara came on some bells of the stemless gentian she got so excited that Caroline quite thought she would be having a lunatic on her hands, but although she pointed this out, Sara was oblivious, not even to be distracted by a great rumbling roar that made Caroline jerk up her head.

"Look, Sara, look!" she cried, pointing to the Eiger. "An avalanche!" That certainly made Sara sit up and take notice, but by the time she had had the spot pointed out to her, the little avalanche was over.

"I expect you imagined it," she remarked. However, to Caroline's satisfaction, the Eiger obliged again very soon, and this time Sara saw, and said "Ooh!" and imagined herself standing right in its path, watching certain death approach and being very brave about it.

They passed through a wood, and were coming out on to a clearing, and Sara was saying, "Well, we haven't seen the waterfall yet. At least, we've seen thousands, but nothing *very* spectacular—" when Caroline gripped her arm and pointed silently to the head of the clearing.

"Gosh, how adorable!" whispered Sara. "What is he, Caro?"

"Chamois, I should think," Caroline whispered back. "Sh! Don't make a sound, and we'll try to get nearer him." But the chamois got wind of them, and with long exquisite bounds disappeared among the trees.

"Oh, gosh," said Sara, "oh, gosh, it's too

much! The mountains, and the gentians and a *chamois.*"

"But no waterfall. And Sara, d'you think these are my two huts?" They had come through a belt of trees to yet another clearing, with two little brown huts perched against the skyline.

"I don't know," said Sara, "it's so different, seen from this angle. You can think they are—that's just as good," but Caroline couldn't agree to this at all.

"Do they call everything chalets?" Sara wanted to know.

"I'm not sure," Caroline was doubtful. "Maybe chalets are where people live. Not like these—these must be cheese-huts or cow-sheds."

"Cheese-huts?"

"M'm. When the cows come up to the high pastures, the cowherds make the milk into cheese. So I read in a book, anyway."

"Now, that's a funny thing! I was wondering what was missing. There *are* no cows."

"No," said Caroline. "I'd noticed that. They must be tucked away somewhere, and only come up to the pastures later. We'll inquire for the cows when we go down."

Sara wandered off, and Caroline sat down on a fence to find her bearings, to see if she could spot the Alpenrose miles below, and to decide if these really were the special huts she had seen from the valley. She looked up once and noticed Sara, flat on her stomach, wriggling towards one of the huts. Caroline smiled to herself, and wondered what role Sara was enacting that made such an ungainly mode of progression necessary. If she had only known, she was being rescued from the most awful fate. Sara actually wasn't very sure if her enemies, somewhere in the trees to her right, were Red Indians (which seemed a little improbable, even to Sara) or a band of mountain brigands, but she knew that Caroline was a prisoner in that hut, and there was only Sara to go to her aid. And she had to go on her tummy, otherwise the brigands' sentry would spot her and shoot her. When she reached the hut she snooped round—and was surprised and gratified to find the door a little open. So she felt quite justified in opening it a little more and slipping inside. What she expected to see, in view of the fact that she shut out all the light by unconsciously pulling the door to behind her, is difficult to say; probably she was still rescuing Caroline. But the hut was pitch dark, and when she pushed the door it would not move.

"Oh, bother it all!" said Sara. "Someone's jammed the door." She threw her weight against it, but it might have been a sparrow's weight for all the effect it had on the door. She paused, and a slow shiver crept up her spine as she thought of the unexplored darkness behind her. *Maybe* it hid cheeses, but maybe mice—or a cow-herd—or even a brigand, who would attack the intruder first and question afterwards. "Calm down," she said to herself firmly: "the hut's empty, I'm *sure* it's empty. Then why was the door open?" she asked herself. "Would it be left open if there was nobody here? Oh, gosh," was all she answered herself, "I wish I could get out!" She lifted up her voice and cried "Ca-a-a-roline!"

Caroline managed to locate the Alpenrose, a ridiculous doll's house beside a narrow ribbon of a road, and wished she could yodel to Vanessa. She practised for a bit, but had to admit that the resultant noises didn't sound much like yodelling. And she watched some more avalanches, and admired the mountains and the softer view down the valley towards Interlaken of trees and pastures and huts. And then she thought of lunch, and, if they were late, of Vanessa pacing up and down in a frenzy, so she reluctantly stirred herself and looked around for Sara. All was silent, and still, and Sara-less.

"*Now* where has she got to?" she wondered, and she climbed a little farther up the path by the side of the trees, calling "Sara!" There was no answering cry. "She can't have gone far," argued Caroline to herself, and she crossed over the green to the far side, to see if Sara were prowling about looking for flowers. Only a steep, tree-clad slope was there. "Lunatic!" Caroline muttered, exasperated, and she went to one of the huts in case Sara had gone to sleep in it, or something. From the other came a series of heavy thumps. "Must be a cow," thought Caroline, in passing; but, as she approached, came another sound, a very faint, plaintive voice shouting "Ca-a-aroline!" "Must be *Sara,*" she thought, hurrying over, doubting her ears. Sure enough, however, when she reached the

door came *Thump!* "Ca–a–aroline!" *Thump!*
"Ca–a—"

"Here I am," she shouted. "What on earth are
you playing at? Come out, you owl—it's time to
go back for lunch."

"I can't *get* out!" Sara's faint pipe was
aggrieved. "The door's jammed."

"Well, maybe it'll teach you not to be such a
nosy little beast," said Caroline.

"What did you say?" Sara shouted.

"Oh, never mind!" Caroline shouted back, and
after walking round the hut she added, "There
don't seem to be any windows. Climb out of the
chimney."

"What?"

"I said, climb out of the chi–i–mney."

"I can't see any chimney," Sara bawled, "and
even if I could, I couldn't."

"Oh, naughty temper!" said Caroline. "All
right, all *right,* stop yelling. I say, listen—"

"Well, I am listening, but you make such silly
suggestions."

"Now I'm serious." Caroline was grinning, but
she put her mouth near the door and shouted,
"When I say ' heave ' you push and I'll pull—"

"When you say what?" Sara wanted to know.

"'*Heave,*'" called Caroline: "—as if it
mattered."

"All right," from Sara.

It was a pity that whenever Caroline pulled Sara
happened to be taking breath—so perhaps not sur-
prisingly the door moved not an inch. After about
half a dozen ineffectual and painful heaves Caroline

felt exhausted, and gave up the struggle, and sat down on the grass by the side of the door to think of something else. Sara, meantime, became so excited that she quite forgot who was supposed to give the signal, and shouting "*Heave* "at the top of her lungs she pushed with all her strength at regular intervals until she thought she would burst.

"One more go," she puffed to herself, and with a cry of "Heave" she hurled herself at the door, which quite unaccountably gave, and Sara pitched headlong through the door like a stone from a sling and went hurtling down the slope.

"Hey!" yelled Caroline. "Look out! You nearly had my ear off!"

Of course they were late for lunch, and Vanessa *was* in a frenzy—but they found the Abbach waterfall on the way back when they weren't even looking for it, and Vanessa calmed down when she saw them, grew worried again when she heard that Sara had been shut up in a cheese-hut, and finally agreed with her that Caroline's conduct had been heartless in the extreme.

Caroline unconcernedly ate her roast veal and salad and grinned at them.

CHAPTER TEN

As they sat in the sun having breakfast next morning, Sara helped herself to enough cherry jam to last a normal person a week, fed surreptitious morsels to the Alpenrose hound, and said, "What's the dog's name, Caro?"

"Towser," suggested Caroline.

"Oh, it couldn't be—!"

Caroline sighed. "It's *too* easy, getting a rise out of you, Sara."

"What d'you feel like doing to-day?" Sara changed the subject.

"Lying on my back in the sun somewhere and sleeping," Caroline answered, poking moodily at her bread and honey and privately longing for some bacon and eggs.

"Gosh, Caro, you lazy pig! You can't possibly sleep all day in *Switzerland*—"

"Oh, can't I? Believe me, I can hardly keep my eyes open. It must be the strong air."

"Strong air, my foot!" Sara said briskly. "It's more likely your natural sloth. No, I think we ought to take our lunch and go off for the whole day—visit the Oberer Gletscher, and maybe get as far as the Grosse Scheidegg. What do you say, Vanessa?"

Vanessa said, "Were you speaking, Sara darling?" Sara gave a little sigh at those vague and lazy cousins of hers, and repeated, with even more ambitious additions, her ideas for a pleasant day.

"But, Sara," objected Vanessa, in a rather shocked voice, "we can't possibly go so far, because John will be arriving some time to-day."

"We can't possibly go so far, because we haven't seven-leagued boots, you mean," said Caroline. "Have you any idea where the Grosse Scheidegg is?" Sara hadn't; she hadn't even any idea what the Grosse Scheidegg was, but she thought it sounded exciting. She lost interest in it a little when Fritz, who came strolling up, told her in reply to her question that it was the saddle-shaped depression which stretched from the Wetter-horn and closed in the top of the valley. She went off with him to discuss walks, while Caroline began to think that a walk and a picnic lunch might be fun—provided that the walk was fairly small, and the lunch was fairly big—and soothed her anxious and dutiful sister. "You ought to know John by this time," she said: "he'll never arrive before midnight. And we should be back by then. Now, you pop off, Vanessa, and ask Frau Berger to make us up a nice lunch, and I'll get hold of Sara." Sara who, as originator of the scheme ought to be taking a more active part, Caroline felt, had completely disappeared, but was at length run to earth in a little shed behind the Alpenrose, watching enthralled as Fritz, who was a ski-instructor in winter, oiled and tended stacks and stacks of skis.

"Fritz has been telling me all about it," she gibbered, as she unwillingly followed Caroline into the hotel to make themselves ready, "and I'm sure I could do it—"

"Do what?" said Caroline.

"Ski, of course—what d'you think I'm talking about?"

Vanessa came in, with three enormous packages which refused to go into the girls' little leather satchels, worn slung over their shoulders; but they tied them on to the strap with string, and so at last were ready to depart.

They had crossed the Lutschine, and had already mounted quite a little way through the trees when Caroline observed, "Your pal seems to have taken a fancy to you, Sara." Sara turned round, and when she discovered that her pal was the Alpenrose dog, trotting quietly along, five yards behind them, she seemed none too pleased.

"Oh, gosh!" she said, as they all stopped and the dog sat down: "we don't want old Towser tagging along with us all the way."

"Well, send him home," said Caroline.

Sara complained that she didn't even know his name, but she did her best by saying in a very fierce voice, "Home, boy, home!" Towser cocked one eye at her affably, and his tail moved slightly, but otherwise he sat where he was.

"Maybe he doesn't know English," said Caroline, and Vanessa, dimly realising that this might be a long job, sat down on a rock.

"But I don't know German!" said Sara, querulously.

"Try French," suggested Vanessa helpfully: "the Swiss are supposed to be bi-lingual."

G

Sara looked a bit doubtful at the "bi-lingual," but obediently ordered Towser in French to take himself off, meantime making threatening movements with her arms and pointing towards the Alpenrose, lying peacefully below them. Towser's expression grew more benign, and his tail moved a little more energetically; but his knowledge of French could not have been much greater than his command of English, for he showed no sign of moving back to Alpenrose.

When her voice began to crack, Sara, whose tones and gestures had been growing wilder and more irate, dropped her arms and turned furiously on her cousins.

"Why don't *you* help?" she demanded.

Caroline looked calmly round for a comfortable rock, and sat down; Towser put his head on his paws and went to sleep.

"Help?" said Caroline. "You're the dog-lover of this party, aren't you?"

"Well, but—" Sara bleated.

"Yes, I know I like dogs, too," Caroline coldly interrupted, "but who made a fuss of Towser ever since we arrived? Who fed him all through breakfast? However," she went on, waving a mouthing Sara to silence, "however, I'll help." She got up, and commanded, "Home, Towser!"

Towser rose, and with one reproachful look, and his tail between his legs, slunk off down the hill.

"All done by kindness," Caroline smiled as they went on.

They mounted a little higher, and Sara almost recovered from her annoyance when they came on some patches of snow (which lay much lower on this side of the valley), and among them a great bank of crocuses, pale mauve, some in the grass, some pushing up through the snow; her recovery was complete when, soon after, noticing a tiny purple flower in the snow, very delicate, very frail, and bending down to identify it triumphantly as soldanella, she glanced down the hill—there, on his haunches, his tongue out, watching them quietly was Towser. They all three sat down then and regarded him, and Vanessa remarked that if she had been expecting so many stops she'd have brought a book. Caroline handed her *Walks and Excursions,* and said, "All right, Towser—you win."

"But what do we do with him?" asked Sara.

"Well," said Caroline, "either you go back to Alpenrose with him—"

"Oh, gosh, Caro—!" began Sara.

"—or else we take him with us, and *you* look after him."

Sara said, "Why me?" but Caroline disregarded that, and eventually Sara decided they should go on and she would be responsible for Towser; and Caroline kindly gave Sara minute instructions about keeping an eye on him and not letting him out of her sight because he probably didn't know this side of the valley at all, and if he got lost might never be seen again. Sara rather guiltily found herself thinking that would be the best thing that could happen, but Towser got into such a state of excitement and pleasure when she patted him and spoke to him that she repented of her harsh thoughts and forgave him for being such a nuisance.

"Don't you think," said Vanessa, "that you might put your dog on a lead, Sara?"

"I do wish you'd stop blaming Towser on to me," said Sara plaintively. "And where d'you imagine I'm going to get a lead? Off a tree?"

"Off your satchel you'd get not a bad substitute," observed Caroline: "that strap detaches. I'll take your bag and your lunch. It's a pity there's no name on his collar." Sara agreed as she snapped the improvised lead on to Towser's collar and wound the other end twice round her hand, and they all settled down again to enjoy their walk.

Not that *that* lasted long, for the next moment Towser smelt an exciting smell and bounded off to see whatever it might be. Sara was jerked off her balance, and landed full length on the hillside, little nose bumped and her glasses sent flying. Caroline laughed and Vanessa admitted that perhaps the lead wasn't such a good idea, and Sara rescued her spectacles and snorted angrily that it was one of the poorest Vanessa had ever had. "And as for Towser," she went on savagely, "he can jolly well take his chance now after such ingratitude, and if he wants to get lost, he can *get* lost."

"Oh, well," said Caroline, "you did your best, I suppose! But you can carry your own lunch now that you haven't Towser to hold on to." And then Towser reappeared, beaming and wagging his tail, the strap dangling uselessly and tripping him up occasionally. He was apparently a reformed character, however, for as they went on he kept by them—darting off now and then to investigate a hut or something, but always bobbing up again.

They circled down the hillside and through Grindelwald; and the Oberer Gletscher, when they reached it, completely restored Sara's faith in glaciers.

"This is something like a glacier," she declared happily, though she was inclined to find the ice-grotto—patiently hollowed out of the solid ice each year, and so blue, so cold—rather eerie, in spite of the little Christmas tree firs placed comically here and there to cheer things up. She left Vanessa and Caroline exclaiming at it, and hurried out into the sunshine again, and went and had a word with the man whose job it was to sit in a little hut and collect the money paid to see the *eisgrotte*. His English was good, as usual, and Sara plied him with questions.

"I've been sadly misinformed about glaciers," said Sara as they went on their way; "I didn't know they could recede."

"I don't know about glaciers, but my tummy will recede if we don't eat soon," said Caroline. "What about it, Vanessa?"

"Gosh, yes!" agreed Sara. "I'm jolly hungry. Let's stop just here."

"What? In the middle of the road?" Vanessa said, and expressed the opinion that it would be nicer to climb up the slopes behind the village and find a good viewpoint of mountains and glacier for a picnic spot. So, protesting, Sara and Caroline plodded on behind her until they found something in views to satisfy her. The ground just there was unfortunately rather sloping, and they had to separate a little to find enough flat ground to give them comfortable seats without sliding downhill; but despite minor discomforts, Sara and Caroline refused to go another step, and unwrapped their packet lunches and began munching while Vanessa was still urging them to go on and find a place that better combined comfort and beauty.

"Oi!" Caroline shouted to Sara, perched somewhere above her. "There's a funny-looking wild flower down here, Sara. Come and have a look at it."

Possibly only a wild flower would have drawn Sara from her lunch at that moment, but draw her it did, and she came slithering down to Caroline, with a sandwich in each hand and another in her mouth.

"Where?" she mumbled.

"Look, there—that black thing."

"Black?" cried Sara, wildly excited, laying a sandwich on the grass as she fumbled in her pocket for her spectacle case, the glasses having been whipped off when she sat down. "Sure you don't mean dark red? Maybe it's nigritella—oh, gosh, I hope it's nigritella! I'd love it to be nigritella— where is it?" pushing on her glasses.

"There, you blind owl, right under your nose."

"*That*?" snorted Sara, cruelly disappointed. "Don't you know what that is? It's a dead clover. Dragging me down here to look at a dead clover!" She glared at Caroline, who only giggled, and picking up her sandwich she went climbing back to her lunch, muttering. A second later her mutterings changed to a roar.

"Towser, you greedy brute, you revolting hound—oh, stop it, get away—*Towser*—!"

"What's all the row about?" called Caroline, clambering up to find out. Sara turned to her a face of defeat and despair.

"It's Towser again," she said in a broken voice: "he's eaten all my lunch!"

Vanessa and Caroline between them managed to produce enough food to save Sara from immediate starvation, but her spirit was broken, and when— after a little sleep in the sun and some further walking, they were on the Terrassenweg returning to Grindelwald and a late tea—repeated calls and whistles failed to bring Towser's honest face to view, she just nodded her head dispiritedly and said, "I knew it. He's really lost this time. All right. I'll go back and look for him—even if I drop."

"He can't be *far* away—" Vanessa said hopefully.

"Oh, yes, he can," interrupted Sara: "you don't know Towser! He's probably half-way up the Faulhorn, or at Grosse Scheidegg by now."

"Cheer up, shrimp," said Caroline. "I'll come with you,"

"And so shall I," said Vanessa.

They went back, right to the very spot where Sara had lost her lunch, and they called and they whistled and they grew more and more tired and more and more cross, but not a hair of Towser was to be seen.

"It's no use," said Vanessa at last. "We'll have to go home, or we'll get no dinner—"

"That would be the last straw," said Sara.

"—and John may be there, wondering where we are.

"Oh," said Caroline, determined to be cheerful, "that dog will turn up all right!"

Sara merely groaned, and they trudged home rather silently.

When they came within sight of Alpenrose, "Oh," cried Vanessa, starting to run, "there's John!"

And "Oh," said Caroline, nudging Sara, "there's Towser!"

CHAPTER ELEVEN

PERHAPS they had found the mountains a little over-powering, and complained that the great big Eiger was just overdone; but next day, when there was no Eiger to be seen, no Wetterhorn, no Metterberg, and the mists rolled round the valley, they regretted their lovely mountains and lamented that they weren't going to be able to show John the beauties of Grindelwald's surroundings straight away.

"But we'll show you the hill path to Grindel this morning," promised Caroline, as they sat at breakfast in the dining-room, "and the village; and we'll have chocolate in an awfully nice little place we discovered."

"I know what we could do this afternoon, seeing it's dull," said Sara: "John could take us down to Interlaken in the car."

"Oh, no!" John said. "Oh, no! I've had enough of motoring for the present, and I don't want to see the inside of a car again for at least a fortnight. You can walk."

"Walk!" said Sara, vexed.

"You seem to have forgotten the little train—" Caroline began mildly, and Sara immediately brightened and said:

"Oh, gosh, *yes!* Let's do that."

So it was decided, and after lunch they caught the two-fifteen, and the nice blue-eyed guard came and passed the time of day with them; and when they reached Interlaken, Sara went quite wild over the shops, and hurried from one window to another, wanting to buy everything; and they found a tea-shop with cakes the like of which they vowed they had never tasted before, and Sara and Caroline—contrary to Vanessa's advice—had four each, besides chocolate and whipped cream. And after that they felt disinclined to do anything but sit very, very quietly. Then, when things had settled down a bit and John had stopped jeering at them, they all departed for Interlaken Ost, and half-way there the rain began—and it poured and it poured, and it poured. They huddled under the lime trees for a little, but that was not much good; so they made a dash for the station at last, and arrived out of breath and very wet and nasty about the legs.

"Just like home," commented Caroline, jerking her head towards the downpour.

"Well," said Vanessa, "I'm only glad we didn't waste a *good* day on Interlaken."

"*Waste* a day on Interlaken!" Sara was amazed at such a point of view. "Interlaken's lovely, Vanessa—and the shops! I'm going to buy presents for simply everybody next time we come down—even you people, and especially John, for bringing me that marvellous camera," and Sara beamed on John, and patted her new camera, and regretted that the weather prevented her taking their photographs there and then.

"When they got up to the Alpenrose the rain had become sleet, and they were all very glad to see the little red-cheeked maid heaving armfuls of wood into the stove in the corner of the sitting-room.

After dinner Fritz came in and told them harrowing tales of foolhardy climbers who had attempted the North Wall of the Eiger—until it was time for Vanessa to force the two girls off to bed, Sara vowing she wouldn't sleep a wink or, if she did, she would have awful nightmares about being lost on the Eiger and hanging suspended from a rope for days.

Caroline thought Sara really was having a nightmare when the most dreadful screeches awakened her near morning. She opened an unwilling eye and saw Sara, in her pyjamas, dancing about by one of the wide-open, unshuttered windows.

"What's the matter?" she growled. "Why don't you shut up? And close that window, you clown—it's freezing!"

"Of course it is, of course it is," Sara crowed. "Oh, do come and look, Caro—it's the loveliest sight you've ever seen!"

Curiosity was too much for Caroline, and struggling into her dressing-gown, she came over to the window and looked out.

"Lumme!" she said. Overnight the valley had become a Christmas-card scene—snow lay deep on the pastures, on the trees, on the roofs of chalets and huts, and even on the apple-blossom outside their window.

"*Isn't* it marvellous?" exulted Sara, as pleased and proud as if solely responsible for this wonder. "Come on, Caroline, let's get dressed and go out."

They had breakfast that morning huddled as close to the dining-room stove as possible; while John talked scathingly of "summer holidays," and

Vanessa and Caroline decided it would be a good chance to write some post-cards.

Two days later, the snow had gone, the sun came out again and the flowers reappeared, and the apple blossom indignantly threw off its load of snow. John marched them up to the Buss Alp, and Sara was very put out to discover that an alp wasn't a mountain at all

From that day on, for each expedition they planned Vanessa wanted to substitute the trip by mountain railway up the Jungfraujoch until, Caroline declared, she became nearly as monotonous as Sara and her parrot cry of "Vienna, Budapest!" Only, Vanessa maintained, her suggestion was at least possible. It was possible, but not just so simple as Vanessa seemed to think. As the railway from Grindelwald to the Kleine Scheidegg was not yet running, to make the trip meant a roundabout journey and a very early start in the morning. Fritz kept assuring them that the weather was not good enough to justify the expense, that there were hurricanes blowing up there, but that he would certainly waken them one morning when it was fine enough. "I really can hardly believe Fritz," Vanessa sighed, looking up into the blue distance, "but I shall have to, I suppose." Meantime there were other expeditions and walks and picnics and the days slipped on, and one Friday morning at breakfast John, amid a shocked silence, said that if they were going to have any hope of catching the ferry on the twenty-ninth, even going home directly through France, they ought to leave on Sunday.

"How foul!" said Sara. "Must we really?

Still, there's always the journey home to look forward to. And if we must leave on Sunday, I think I'll pop up to Grindel this morning and buy some presents for people." Sara had been restrained from wholesale buying only by force on occasion, so now Caroline felt she might relax her rigid discipline, and they set off together, leaving Vanessa and John still discussing plans for the last day or two.

"I thought you were going to buy all your presents in Interlaken," Caroline observed to Sara as they approached the village.

"I'm going to buy *some* there," Sara put her right, "but I'm getting Daddy a musical cigarette box, and I don't want to have to carry that up from Interlaken playing tunes all the way."

In front of the shops the long trestles lay as usual covered with their array of knick-knacks.

"But when you really get down to it," Caroline pointed out, "there seems to be nothing but carved bears—bears hugging ash-trays to their chests, clothes-brushes in the shape of bears, bear brooches—"

"There's an eagle," Sara pointed out annoyingly, "and a chamois—the pet! And, anyway, there are plenty of musical things, rows and rows of them. Let's try the tunes." She opened the lid of a cigarette box, and, to her delight, as the little tinkling tune struck up, the cigarettes slowly rose to view. "*Isn't* that fun!" she said.

Caroline picked up another, and, as it began to play, something, as she said afterwards, seemed to come over her, and into the eye of Caroline, the

controlled, the placid Caroline, who hated scenes
and fuss and bother, came a wicked gleam, and
she went mad. As fast as her fingers would work
she picked up fruit-dishes and up-ended them, she
opened the lids of boxes, she turned musical bowls
upside-down—and as each one began to play its
different tune the peaceful air of Grindelwald was
rent with discord. Sara giggled, and got busy herself; but when the shocked, alarmed face of the
shopkeeper popped out of the door, she gave a little
squeal and said, "Gosh, *Caroline*—!" and
Caroline, who, she maintained later, meant just to
hear the effect of them all together and then put
them back, lost her nerve completely and crying,
"Run, Sara, *run*!" took to her heels down the
street, with a half-scared, half-laughing Sara
puffing along behind her.

When they came towards their favourite little
cafe, two figures rose from one of the tables outside,
and made to intercept them.

"Lumme, we're caught!" gasped Caroline.
Sara took one look at the couple, gave a wail of
distress, and, seizing Caroline's hand urged her on,
while the pair waved and called and stared after
the fleeing figures. Caroline, belatedly recognising
them, cried, "Stop, Sara! stop, you ass: it's the
couple we met on the Townsend Ferry—they're not
after us," but Sara, her mind full of her guilty and
forgotten transaction on the Drachenfels moaned:
"I *daren't*!"

But Caroline had returned to her right mind; she
forced Sara to stop, and waited, panting, rather
embarrassed, for the two to approach. They came

up, and Blondie smiled very brightly and said, "Well you *do* seem in a hurry! But *how* extra-ordinary, seeing you again, here of all places!"

Caroline smiled uncertainly and said fatuously: "How do you do? It's a small world, isn't it?" And Sara groaned silently to herself and thought it was a jolly lot *too* small.

"I was longing to meet you people again," the woman chattered on, "for, d'you know, at Calais I lost a book, and I've been wondering ever since if by *any* chance I dropped it in your car? When I came over to talk to you, do you remember? I'm almost sure I had it then, and—"

"My wife values that book very highly," the man's hard, rasping voice cut it, "for sentimental reasons."

Sara said to herself, "Oh, gosh!" and Caroline said, "Oh, yes, you did, as a matter of fact—we were wondering how it got into our car. You've got the book, haven't you, Sara?"

And Sara swallowed, crossed her fingers and said very faintly, "Yes," and, since she knew she was blushing like anything, wished the husband would stop staring at her.

"*Isn't* that lucky!" Blondie beamed on them. "But," and she gave a little laugh, "I don't sup-pose you carry it about with you, do you?"

"The woman's nuts," thought Caroline, but aloud she gave a polite laugh, and said, "Oh, no! It's at our hotel, the Alpenrose, isn't it, Sara?"

Sara said "Yes" even more faintly, and crossed her fingers again, and then thought that for the remainder of this singularly unpleasant conversation she had better keep them crossed. Blondie was saying vivaciously that they would come along and collect it, and Caroline was saying they mustn't think of that, she and Sara would bring it to them in the afternoon, and Blondie said, "Well, do come and have tea with us here—it'll be so nice to have some English people to talk to again!"

"We're Scots," said Caroline, more for something to say than anything else.

"Oh, really?" said Blondie, bored. "How interesting. Now, we'll see you this afternoon, and you can tell us the things in Grindelwald we simply mustn't miss, for we have only just arrived and we haven't much time to spend. We'll see you here then—ask for us if we aren't sitting outside—"

"Er—" began Caroline.

"My dear, of course! How stupid of me! We don't know each other's names, do we? *Have* you a card, darling? I find I *never* have a card when I want one," and the man took out a pocket-book and handed over a visiting-card, while Caroline—feeling at a decided disadvantage in this exchange of civilities, and wishing that Sara wouldn't be such a dumb fish—mumbled awkwardly that she was Caroline Storm and this, indicating the dumb fish, was her cousin Sara. Sara, perhaps feeling that something was expected of her, but desperate to get the conversation away from books, suddenly pointed to the grey Armstrong-Siddeley standing by the kerb and said:

"Is that you car?"

Blondie, looking rather put out at this abruptness but still determined to be jolly, said, "Oh, yes, we have—"

"I thought it was yellow," interrupted Sara.

There was a sudden tiny pause. Then the man's harsh voice said, "My wife wanted it changed—"

"My dear, *yes,*" the flood of Blondie's chatter broke in, "the dust on those Continental roads! It was driving me frantic, for if there's one thing I do insist on, it's a nice, clean, tidy-looking car. But imagine your noticing! This grey is such a boon—Now you *won't* fail us this afternoon? We'll be so looking forward to it." And after some more smiles and vivacity on the part of the lady, the girls were free to go. They made a false start along the street, and then backed hastily when Caroline remembered her misdemeanours over the musical boxes. "We'll circle round the low way by Grund, and avoid the shop," said Caroline. As they re-passed the cafe, the couple, who had sat down again, stared, but Blondie waved heartily. The girls hurried down the road.

"Think of those two bobbing up again," mused Caroline. "What's their name—Burton-Ware, with a hyphen—Christmas! You know, Sara, I think they're queer. Did you see the way he stared at you, never took his eyes off you once? And Blondie was blooming bright, wasn't she?" Sara did not reply. "And," Caroline went on, "*I* didn't want to have tea with them, but what could I do? We'll give 'em back the old book, and that'll be the end of it."

Sara groaned. Caroline looked at her and said, "What's the matter with *you*?"

"It won't be the end of it," said Sara in a hollow voice.

"Why not? I don't want to see either of them again: we'll just return the book and have a cup—"

"I haven't got the book," said Sara.

"*What?*" exclaimed Caroline. "But you were reading it; what did you do with it?"

"I gave it to a man on the Drachenfels," said Sara. Caroline stopped dead and stared at her.

"What on earth for?" she asked.

"A lemonade," said Sara, pink to the ears, and the whole story came out.

"Well," said Caroline, when she had heard all and had told Sara what she thought of her for swigging lemonade on the quiet while the rest of them were dying of thirst, "this is a fine kettle of fish. This is serious, Sara. What *will* Mrs. Burton-Ware say when we go back and tell her?"

"What will Mr. Burton-Ware say?" asked Sara, in despair.

"'My wife values that book very highly,'" mimicked Caroline.

"I feel sick," said Sara.

"Cheer up, shrimp—it won't be so bad. I wonder if we ought to go back now and get it over?"

"Oh, *no*," Sara gasped, "Caroline, *please*—!"

"All right, keep calm. I think the best thing to do is for you to write to your Drachenfels friend with some money and ask him to send on the book to Mrs. Burton-Ware's London address whenever you get back to Alpenrose. And then when we see them this afternoon we can tell them. At least you will have tried."

Sara began to recover her spirits. "And maybe John will come with us, for I'm sure that man will kill me when I say I haven't got it."

"Why d'you think they're making such a fuss about it?" Caroline puzzled.

"Maybe they've committed a murder and that book is the only clue," suggested Sara, her thriller-fed imagination beginning to function again. "I'm sure he's capable of anything."

"If it was that, they'd be jolly *glad* to be rid of it, I should imagine," Caroline jeered.

"Not if I was thinking of taking it to the police or someone who would know it was the only clue, like a private detective with a sixth sense," maintained Sara. "And he certainly looked at me as if he suspected me of *knowing too much*. Have there been any murders in the newspapers recently—don't think we've seen a paper since we left home."

Caroline was becoming a bit bored by the subject, but Sara's mention of newspapers made her stop short again in the middle of the road; and, clutching Sara's arm with a grip that made that unfortunate yelp with pain, she said in a conspiratorial tone:

"Sara! The Phillimore diamonds!"

"Gosh!" said Sara, taking Caroline and her damaged arm very seriously. "You don't mean to say that you think that book has something to do with the diamonds? And I gave it away for a glass of—"

Caroline had not, actually, thought anything of the kind, but now the suggestion was made, it seemed a good one.

"Well, I don't know," she interrupted thoughtfully. "These people seemed—wrong, somehow. They're making a great song and dance about a book—and if it's of such sentimental value, why cart it all over the Continent? And yet they must want it badly or they'd never have come away up to Grindelwald after us—was it very valuable *looking*? Old or anything?"

"Gosh, no! And maybe they were coming in any case," said Sara, forced to bring up the point, but longing to have it answered.

"If they had been, surely Mrs. Burton-Ware would have mentioned it—she's friendly enough, now. And then there's the car—the dust question would have occurred to any one in their senses before. And any normal people, I should have thought, would wait till they got home before having their car repainted."

Sara had stopped paying attention. "If this was my one chance of having a real adventure!" she groaned. "If that book was stuffed full of diamonds! And I gave it away for a glass of lemonade!"

"*Was* it stuffed full of diamonds?" asked Caroline.

"Don't be dotty!"

"No. It couldn't be, of course. But I do think

there might be a connection between the book and the robbery."

"But," said Sara, torn between a desire to believe that there wasn't, and that it did not matter about her rotten bargain, and that there very definitely *was*, and she had thrown away a never-to-be-repeated opportunity of touching adventure at last, "what could a priceless diamond necklace have to do with *Tales of Mystery*?"

"I don't know," sighed Caroline. "I say, what's got into John? For they were within sight of Alpenrose now, and John was out on the road, gesticulating madly.

"Hurry *up!*" they heard him cry as soon as they were within earshot. "Do hurry up. Where have you been?" he said, as they came running up.

"You know where we've been," said Caroline, aggrieved. "In Grindelwald. What's—"

"Well, never mind that," fussed John. "We have decided to go up the Jungfraujoch, and stay the night there, and lunch is ready, and we thought you would never come and that we should miss the train."

"Oh, gorgeous!" said Sara. "Fancy us going up to the highest point of any railway line in Europe! And all the mountains and ice and snow. Could I take skis, Caro, do you think?"

Over lunch John and Vanessa told them that Fritz had at last agreed that the weather looked settled enough for the expedition to be worth while, but by that time it was too late to complete the round in one day, so they had decided to blow the expense, do it in comfort, and spend the night at the hotel there.

"Now," said John, "about money," and he took out his little black book where he meticulously noted down expenses. "It's rather dear, the train and everything, and we *must* keep enough for getting home. So to make sure of *that,* we'll each take sufficient for the night, and we'll leave the remainder with Fritz, for I don't want you all to go spending recklessly" —and he fixed his eye on Sara — "and then find we can't get home. Now go and fetch your money, and collect a toothbrush or whatever you need, and a heavy coat, and *be quick*—we mustn't miss that train."

So Sara hastily swallowed a last bite of bread and cheese, and they dashed off to get ready, and the only thing that was worrying Sara was a feeling at the back of her mind that there was something she ought to be doing.

When they were in the train Sara remembered.

"Oh, gosh, Caroline," she said, "the Burton-Wares!"

"Whew!" Caroline gave a dismayed whistle. "That's torn it! I completely forgot."

"Caroline, they'll be *furious.* John, *what* shall I do?"

"If you would just confide in me what the trouble is, I might possibly be able to tell you," John said.

"Well, it's those beastly Burton-Wares," said Sara helpfully. "And they want that book and I haven't it and actually *we* think they're murderers and their name isn't Burton hyphen Ware or

Blondie at all, but Slippery Sam and Nasty Nellie or something, and I know they'll kill me—"

"Sara, *darling!*" interrupted Vanessa in an alarmed voice, and poor John looked so completely bewildered that Caroline had to laugh, and explain more coherently what had happened.

"And seriously, John," she finished, "I do think there's something awfully odd about them. I think we should go home by Rhondorf, collect that book ourselves, and see what's in it."

"But Caroline," said John humouring her, "Sara read it, didn't she? Was there anything funny about it, Sara?"

"No-o-o," Sara had to admit. "But," she went on eagerly, "it would be in code."

"What would—the bloodstains?"

"Ha, ha !" said Caroline, unamused. "But the Phillimore diamonds were stolen the night before the customs were making such an examination— *you* remember, and those cuttings which were in *Tales of Mystery* were all about it—we thought they were there because the Burton-Wares were interested—"

"Surely," said Vanessa, "no self-respecting burglar would cut out the accounts of his own crime and leave them in the principal clue for any one to see? Even I—"

"But they *do*," Sara assured her earnestly. "All the detective stories tell you how the master-crooks are so cocky when they have planned the perfect crime that they do all sorts of things they think the police are too stupid to notice."

"It's the only way they get caught," Caroline contributed.

"Well, I think that's making it all just too simple for the police," said John. "And Caroline, I'm surprised at you letting yourself be carried away by Sara's ideas."

The train's arrival at Interlaken put a stop to any discussion this remark might have led to; for they had decided, having some time to wait for the train up the Lauterbrunnen valley which would join the Jungfraujoch railway, to spend that time in Interlaken rather than at Zweilutschinen, where the two railways met.

"Now, chaps," said John, "you can do what you like—but be at that little tea-place, you know, where you stuffed before, in three-quarters of an hour."

When John and Vanessa arrived at the rendez-vous they were astonished to find Caroline already there. At least they thought it was Caroline, but she was so hidden by newspapers it was difficult to be certain. John struggled through the jungle, and cleared a couple of chairs for Vanessa and himself, while Caroline scanned a newspaper hastily, page by page, tossed it aside, seized another.

"What *are* you looking for?" he said. "And why all the old English newspapers—May 3rd, 4th —Caroline, explain yourself."

Caroline looked up impatiently. "I'm looking to see if there is anything more about the Phillimore robbery, of course—and did I have a hunt for all those papers! All over Interlaken. You take this

pile, Vanessa—I haven't been through them yet—
and John, you take those."

Vanessa murmured something about wanting her
tea, but there was no gainsaying Caroline.

"I say," said John indignantly, "this one's all
sticky!"

Caroline said absently, "Oh, yes—I dropped a
cake on that—"

"Cake?"

"Yes, I had to have something to sustain me."

John sighed, and remarked that at this rate there
was no knowing when he would get something to
sustain him—when suddenly Caroline shouted (and
the other people in the tea-shop, who were looking
at this mad English company anxiously, jumped a
little in their chairs):

"Got it! Listen, you two. It's May 6th—four
days after the Phillimore robbery.

"The police," she read, "are anxious to trace
the owner of an Armstrong-Siddeley car which was
seen by a workman returning home late on the night
of May 2nd, outside the village of Stanmere, where
the house of Mr. J. Johnston Phillimore is situated.
The witness, who has just come forward, did not
observe the number of the car, but he states that it
was painted a pale yellow colour. Scotland Yard is
of the opinion that the owner of this car may be
able to assist them in their inquiries into the loss of
the Phillimore necklace—"

"—and then there's a great long screed about the

necklace again, but we know all that. Well, that proves it, doesn't it?"

Vanessa, who was not clever with newspapers, was valiantly trying to fold them away, and really only succeeded in becoming more like a cocoon every minute. She peered out of her shell worriedly, and said, "Proves *what*, Caroline, darling?"

"Lumme," said Caroline elegantly, "didn't we tell you about Slippery Sam's car? He's had it painted grey!"

"And what was it before?' asked John: "red with purple spots?"

"It was a pale yellow Armstrong-Siddeley," said Caroline.

"Was it, by Jove!" John was startled. "I—"

"Here comes the object," interrupted Caroline, nodding towards the street. "Look at it!"

The object was hurrying along with little trotting steps, her chestnut curls dancing, her glasses slipping down her nose, parcels and packages bulging her blazer pockets and hanging from every finger.

"Tut," John made a testy noise, "she's mad! Does she mean to carry all that stuff up to the Jungfraujoch?"

But, Sara assured him (when she got her breath back and her cakes chosen) with difficulty, she didn't at all intend to carry her purchases further than Interlaken Ost; there she was going to leave them, tied together, and collect them on the way home.

"You were very quick, buying that lot," remarked Caroline. "Not your usual at all."

"Well, I had decided before, really, what to buy for everybody, and I had a good idea, from last time we were here, you know, where to go."

"Good gracious," John suddenly exclaimed, "look at the time! Must be going. Will you two give me your money now, and I'll push on and buy the tickets."

There was a sudden, hideous silence as Sara opened her purse and produced a ten-franc note.

"That seems to be all I have left," she said, in a frightened small voice....

After a little Caroline gathered sufficient strength to say, rather pleadingly, "You have enough in reserve to finance her, haven't you, John?"

"No," said John, "I haven't. After working it out and telling you what to bring, *I* brought about a hundred and fifty francs extra; but that's no good —we *might* manage, but I don't know to a franc what the hotel will cost, and supposing we got up to Jungfraujoch and couldn't pay the bill? No, I'm afraid we must abandon it."

Sara was feeling like a traitor, but she just stared at her half-eaten cake in silence. She was longing to say how terribly sorry she was, but was afraid that if she tried to speak she would disgrace herself completely. No one knew quite *what* to say. John was wishing vehemently to himself that he had insisted, as he wanted to do, on taking control of all the money—but no, he thought, Sara and Caroline *must* be independent. Vanessa was thinking that when she went outside and saw the Jungfrau in all her shining and remote—very remote—beauty, she would most certainly do Sara an injury.

"Sara," she suddenly burst out savagely, "I could push you into the lake."

Such an unusually bloodthirsty sentiment coming from their sweet-tempered Vanessa cleared the air considerably. Caroline laughed and said, "Which d'you fancy, Sara, for your grave, Thun or Brienz?"

John said, "I'll hold her down, with pleasure."

Sara said, "Oh, Vanessa darling, I'd *jump* in both lakes if I thought it would do any good. I'm terribly, *terribly* sorry. There was the money, and it just seemed to disappear. And I completely forgot there was no more. Couldn't you people go up the Jungfraujoch and I'll go back to Alpenrose?"

"That's not to be thought of, naturally," said John.

"No," exclaimed Vanessa dramatically." It's fate. I shall never see the Jungfrau."

"Well, but look here," said Caroline, "why not go back to Alpenrose to-day—we have to now, anyway—and leave to-morrow instead of Sunday, take the car as far as we can—that's Lauterbrunnen, isn't it—and do the Jungfraujoch on the way home?"

"Caroline," said Vanessa in admiration, "you're the only one among us with any common sense."

So, when it seemed that this scheme might be feasible, every one cheered up; Caroline told Sara about the piece in the paper, and Sara was so excited she had another cake—although she did try

to make out it was in case Frau Fritz hadn't anything in for dinner.

Frau Fritz did have something in for dinner; and
Fritz seemed very amused, but very glad, to have
them back so soon.

"Some friends called to see you when you were
gone two hours," he said. "I tell them you are
gone, and they are very set-up—"

"Very set-up?" queried Caroline, intrigued, and
muttered to John, "You see, they came after us.
What d'you mean, set-up?"

"Very angry and excited—"

"Oh, *upset*!"

"*Ja*, set-up. But when I say you come back
to-morrow, all smiles, and they say they will come
again in the morning. And they are so pleased with
my little Alpenrose—they will come to live here,
they say, and they ask to see the rooms, and I show
them—"

"There you are," said Caroline triumphantly to
John, and not paying much attention to Fritz's
latter remarks, "I *told* you they were making more
fuss than one book was worth."

"Oh, gosh," Sara said to any one who would
listen, "if *only* they could be crooks—real live
crooks! It would make up for the Jungfraujoch
and everything."

Vanessa looked at her solemnly for a moment and
then, "No, Sara," she finally said, "I really can-
not agree with you there."

CHAPTER TWELVE

IT seemed to Sara that she had only been asleep for about two seconds that night, when she woke and opened her eyes.

"Whatever is John doing in our bedroom?" she wondered, half-asleep. "What are you looking for, John?" she said aloud, sitting up. And then "John" behaved very queerly indeed, as it struck Sara as she peered into the half-light. He spun round from the dressing-table where he was crouching and darted for the window.

"Gosh!" yelled Sara. "It's not John! Help! Burglars!" and without stopping to think she leapt out of bed and dived for the intruder's legs. But he had had too great a start: one of his legs was over the sill, and, as Sara reached him, his other foot came swiftly up and, whether by accident or design, caught her full on the temple. She dropped, without a sound, to the floor.

But the noise had been too much for Caroline, sound sleeper as she was. She came to in time to see Sara fall, and a leg disappear. Calling "John! Van! Herr Berger! Help!" she made for the window and leaned out. There was a moon, and she saw, before a bend in the road hid him, the running figure of a man; Towser, locked somewhere in an outhouse, was barking madly but faintly; Fritz appeared and ran up the road in the direction Caroline indicated.

Behind her, the bedroom door burst open, and John, with tousled hair and sleepy eyes, came in, and snapped on the light, demanding furiously: "What is the meaning of this disgusting uproar?" Vanessa was behind him, and, when she saw Sara lying on the floor, began babbling excitedly. Caroline turned round and, nearly stepping on the prostrate Sara, imperiously motioned them to silence. "Sh-sh!" she said: in the amazed hush which followed there could be heard in the distance the sound of a car's engine. "D'you hear that car?" she asked. "D'you hear that peculiar whine? It's an Armstrong-Siddeley, it's the self-changing gear —isn't it, John?"

"Sounds like it," John agreed. "But what—"

"Well, the Burton-Wares have an Armstrong— that horrible man got wind-up about his book, and came here to help himself—she had the car up the road in readiness for the get-away."

"But—" began John again, when a little moan from the unfortunate Sara, who might have been lying there yet, so absorbed were the others in this new aspect of the burglar, interrupted him. She sat up dazedly, her hand to her head.

"They got me, pal!" she whispered.

Vanessa, contrite, flew to her side, and with John's help, heaved her sturdy little body on to her bed.

"Get something, Caroline, quick—smelling salts, brandy, sal volatile," Vanessa dithered; but Sara was quite conscious, lying regarding her hand.

"Gosh!" she said, in mingled terror and gratification, "Gosh, blood! I've been shot!"

"No, no," soothed Vanessa, "he only hit you with something—there's a wee cut on the side of your forehead, and it's bleeding a little."

"A wee cut!" said Sara in disgust. "I *feel* as if I had been shot."

Caroline reappeared with hot water, followed by Fritz, bearing an enormous first-aid box; and excusing himself politely to Vanessa, he, well-used to administering first-aid on the ski-ing fields, took command of Sara. The others stood round in silence and watched him bathe and dress the cut, but when Sara put up her hand and felt what he had done, she said:

"Oh, I say! A measly bit of sticking plaster! Can't I have a bandage?"

Fritz smiled, and as he was wrapping a useless bandage round Sara's head, he said to John, "He escape, the thief, in an auto—I did not see it, it was round the corner, but I hear it. I am so very sorry this has happened—"

"Oh, don't worry—it's not your fault, Herr Berger," John said. "I don't understand it at all—"

"Well, I do," Caroline interrupted vigorously. "It's as plain as a pikestaff what happened. Wait till I show you these cuttings—"she foraged in a drawer and produced them. "Now read those—they give a fuller account than the paper we had in Calais." John meekly took them and glanced over them.

"This doesn't add up to much," he said.

"No, but everything together *does,*" Caroline insisted. "Listen: this is what I think happened— I've been working it out. These two, Slippery Sam and Nasty Nellie, did this robbery—the night before we sailed, please note—and the book, in *some* way, is mixed up with it. Then at the Calais customs— *and* remember the customs man told us they were taking extra precautions because of a jewel robbery—Nasty Nellie took fright, planted the book on us—"

"Our car was *miles* behind theirs," Sara, looking very rakish with her bandage dipping over one eye, sat up and contributed before Vanessa gently pushed her down again.

"—yes," went on Caroline, speaking very fast to get her tale out before John could stop her and send her back to bed, "they would naturally expect to finish first: then, when they had been okayed, she would come casually up and say, 'Oh, did I drop a book in your car,' and off she'd go. But when we got away before them they were stumped—so they followed us here—"

"How did they know we were here?" John thought he had a trump-card this time. Sara sat up.

"Because I told her on the boat," she said, and lay down again. Caroline heaved a great sigh of relief.

"Yes, of course, I forgot—and Sara also said we were going to Paris and Geneva, so maybe they wasted some, time going there, besides the time it would take to have their car repainted. Then, when they saw us running away, to-day, and Sara

I

was so queer, they thought we must have tumbled to something, for they couldn't know Sara's funny behaviour was for another reason altogether—"

"That's where the colossal vanity of the crook trips him up," said the master-mind from the bed.

"—and when we didn't turn up for tea that must have just about put the lid on it. Probably they then went to the other Alpenrose to look for us, and they would think we were misleading them delibe-rately, and so they came panting down here."

"They came in an auto," said Fritz, deeply interested in the story, not half of which made sense to him, but anxious for accuracy.

"Yes, and when they learned we'd gone," Caro-line swept on, "they nearly had a heart-attack. But when they heard we were only gone for the night, they trumped up this story about liking the hotel, and asked to see the rooms so that they could have a look round. There was no sign of the book, of course, but they were able to locate our bed-rooms. They would decide to come back to-night, when the rooms were supposed to be empty. And John, what we have to do is to start off at *once* for Rhondorf and get that book." And, quite over-come by the longest speech she had ever made in her life, she collapsed exhausted at the feet of Sara, who again sat up and shook her solemnly by the hand.

"You took the very words out of my mouth," she said.

If the words had come out of Sara's mouth, John would have paid them scant attention: coming from

Caroline, common-sensical Caroline, they shook him. But he rallied.

"Don't you think that these people—what's their name? Burton-Ware? Merciful goodness—are a perfectly normal couple who are trying to be friendly—"

"Gosh," said Sara, "I don't call hitting me a conk on the head very friendly!"

"Goodness, no!" exclaimed Vanessa.

"No," John admitted. "And it certainly sounded like an Armstrong engine which removed the burglar, and they aren't exactly thick as blackberries in Grindelwald at this time of year. No, by jove!" and he slapped his knee, "it *is* extremely queer behaviour to go barging into people's bedrooms in the middle of the night, and if it is the book they're after, it must be worth a lot to risk that for it—"

"You read it, Sara," interrupted Vanessa; "were there any pearls sticking out of it?"

"No, of course not," said Sara. "You don't expect to find pearls in a book, do you?"

"Well, really, by now I don't know what I'm to expect," said Vanessa rather pathetically.

"And, anyway," added Sara, "they were diamonds."

John frowned on these interruptions. "Be quiet, you two; and sit down, everybody. Sara, you lie down. Now, supposing we do go to Rhondorf to get a hold of this book, we needn't go any sooner than we planned—"

Caroline, who had been rapidly explaining to Fritz the bits in the story, and they were numerous, which he could not quite follow, broke off to exclaim, "John, how utterly ridiculous! We'll have to leave first thing in the morning, for we simply couldn't face them again without admitting we haven't the book."

"I shouldn't think they could face *us* after to-night's carry-on," growled Sara.

"Be quiet, Sara," said Caroline; "we must get this thing settled. How soon d'you think they'll be after us again in the morning, John?"

"Well, they're still supposed to be ordinary people on holiday and on the best of terms with us, so I expect they'll leave a decent interval for us— or you, rather—to show up in Grindelwald, and then when you don't, they'll come down here— about eleven, should you think?"

"So we had better leave here about nine?"

"Oh, earlier, earlier. We can't expect too much from the old Major, you know, and we must get a good start. Six o'clock, we'll leave."

John's motto, now that he had given in to Sara's and Caroline's argument, seemed suddenly to have become, "In for a penny, in for a pound!" and Vanessa listened aghast to her husband making plans which even to her wifely ears sounded utterly fantastic. This last, however, struck her as just overdoing it.

"I never heard anything so silly," she said, with unusual decision. "Here's Sara, not half an hour recovered from unconsciousness, and you propose to career her all over Europe without allowing her even a decent night's rest first: it's half-past one now, and it will be goodness knows what time before you get into bed again—"

"All over Europe!" snorted John.

"Old Sara's never any more than semi-conscious at the best," Caroline grinned, and Sara sat up with a venomous look in her one visible eye; but before anything could be said, Caroline hurried on. "But perhaps Van's right, John. By the time we pack and everything."

"Yes, perhaps eight o'clock will do. We'll get Herr Berger to lay a false trail—you'll do that, won't you?" Fritz looked puzzled, but nodded his head, and Caroline giggled and said joyfully,

"Oh, gorgeous, *yes*! We'll send them up the Jungfraujoch—"

"And to Vienna and Budapest," muttered Sara. "But I say," she said, in alarm, a thought striking her, "we're not going to let them get away completely, are we? We must capture them and deliver them over to Scotland Yard."

This was a new aspect, and rather a tricky one, John felt, suddenly sobering down. It was one thing to play treasure hunts from Grindelwald to Rhondorf to please Caroline and Sara, even if the treasure proved no more exciting than a book, of sentimental value to Mrs. Burton-Ware, but it was quite another to start accusing the Burton-Wares of being really Slippery Sam and Nasty Nellie, crooks and jewel thieves, without the faintest shadow of actual proof—*quite* another thing to be getting involved with the police in a foreign country and probably finding themselves on the wrong side of the bars in the end.

"Oh, well, Sara," he said cautiously, after these thoughts had visited him and left him a little apprehensive, "we don't really know if we have any case against them yet—we can't do anything about that until we've had a look at this book, you know."

"Oh, John!" said Caroline, disgusted at such feebleness.

"Oh, *John*!" said Sara, in an agony lest her long-cherished dream of nonchalantly handing over a bunch of crooks to Scotland Yard was to be denied fulfilment by over-caution on John's part. "Of course we know they're crooks, and the book will prove it, somehow. And look—if we don't lay too false a trail, just enough to give us sufficient start to collect the evidence in Rhondorf, *then* we could have them arrested when they make up on us?"

"I'm having no dealings with foreign policemen if I can help it," said John, with a firmness which brooked no argument. "With the language difficulty and so on, you never know where you'll land."

"Well, look here," Sara was becoming desperate, "how about this for a scheme? These people will come down here, and you, Herr Berger, will say we decided to go a day or two sooner, and we were so sorry to miss them, and they'll be furious—they'll ask you where we've gone, Herr Berger, and you'll pretend to be not too willing to tell them, won't you—?"

"I have done so," Fritz promised, rather cryptically.

"—and then they'll offer you a tremendous bribe—at least, I should in their place." Sara went on, warming up, "and you, with a great show of reluctance, will finally take it"—Fritz's eyes crinkled up and he grinned—" and you'll tell them we've gone up the Jungfraujoch, and then we're going to Geneva for a night and then through—Paris will do, and that we're crossing to England on the twenty-ninth. If they're really harmless people they won't think of bribing Herr Berger, they'll just wait for us to post on to them the book, for we have their address; but if they're crooks, they'll chase us, and they'll be right off our route, and we'll evade them till we reach Dover, and by that time we'll have the evidence, and be on English soil where the policemen are wonderful," and Sara lay back, breathless.

"M'm, that's not too bad," said Caroline, critically. "But wouldn't they be crazy to risk crossing back to England when once they are safe on the Continent?"

"What's the good of being safe if they haven't the swag?" Sara asked. "And surely fifty thousand pounds' worth of diamonds are worth a little bit of a risk? Besides," she added, "they can never be quite sure whether we're wise to their game or just dumb."

("Can't we go to bed now?" Vanessa moaned.)

"No, that's a point," John admitted. "And that seems not at all a bad plan. It doesn't commit us to anything until we gain possession of the book; and *if* we find anything we could communicate with Scotland Yard, and they could have a bobby waiting at Dover. Of course it all depends if Herr Berger will agree? "and he turned politely to Fritz.

But there was no difficulty there, for Fritz by this time was completely hypnotized by all this talk of diamonds and crooks and the utter conviction of Sara and Caroline, and was ready to agree to anything; and they fixed up all the details and arranged to be called at six-thirty—in spite of Caroline's tentative suggestions that seven really would be early enough—and it seemed as though at last everybody would get to bed. Vanessa and John and Fritz departed, with John solemnly instructing Sara to go to sleep immediately, and daring her to speak another word or she'd have brain fever and would have to be left behind, to fall into the clutches of Nasty Nellie; and Sara thought that that might be quite exciting, but on the whole not so much fun as going with them, and promised to *try* and sleep at once.

And Vanessa, as she went out, murmured sadly, "The Jungfraujoch!" but no one heard her.

CHAPTER THIRTEEN

THE next morning was warm and sunny as they left the Alpenrose, to every one's surprise more or less, at the time agreed on.

Sara was waving vigorously out of the rear window to Herr Fritz and his Frau, and saying, "If we weren't going on such an exciting journey I should be in tears now at leaving Fritzy and the dear Alpenrose."

"Just see if my hat's there, Sara, will you? And that the luggage is safely on."

"Oh, I expect it's all right *this* time," Sara said cheekily: "it was Fritz who strapped it on. And here's your hat. And, oh, Caroline, I've just remembered—I haven't got Daddy's musical cigarette-box! I've something for every one else and nothing for him. John," she called, "do you think you could stop in Interlaken for a minute or two?"

"Gracious, Sara, you can't want chocolate and cakes so early in the day, surely," asked John. Sara explained. "I'm going to get petrol, so you can have three minutes," he promised then. "But that's all you may buy"; he added, "I don't want to run out of money and have to sit somewhere on the roadside waiting for Slippery Sam to come up and relieve us of the diamonds."

"Every time I hear you mention diamonds or Two-gun Willie or Nasty Nessie," complained

137

Vanessa, "I feel sick. Couldn't we just pretend we're making our way peacefully to—wherever we are making our way—" she finished helplessly.

"Nasty *Nellie,* Vanessa dear, not Nessie," said Sara earnestly.

John laughed and said, "That'll do, Sara; admire the scenery now for a bit."

At Interlaken, Sara got her musical box and John got his petrol.

"As long as we're in Germany before the banks close for the week-end there's no particular hurry, so I think we ought to vary things as much as we can and go by Lucerne, Zurich, and Lake Constance," he said.

Caroline and Sara, desperate to get to Rhondorf and *Tales of Mystery,* were inclined to demur, but Vanessa was only too thankful John hadn't gone quite so violently mad as they had, and insisted on the Constance route being taken.

"It won't delay us much," John assured the girls, and turning to the garage man he discussed roads and routes with him, and asked how soon he thought they might expect to be in Baden, going via Constance.

"Ulm—Stuttgart would be quicker," suggested Caroline, but John, to please Vanessa, thought the other would be better for scenery.

"Ask him when we'll reach Bonn," said Caroline. "This man is wonderful—he knows everything, and his English is terribly good."

"Constance it is," said John, when the discussion was over. "Since we have to go home mainly the same way as we came, the more variety we can fit in the better."

So the girls accepted this decision and were forced to admit that as far as scenery went it was a sensible one—" If only we had time, or inclination, to bother about scenery *now,*" as Sara kept muttering to Caroline. To Vanessa's disgust they scarcely spared the Alps more than a glance as they saw the last of them across Lake Constance.

"Yes, they *are* gorgeous, and I hate leaving them," sighed Sara; then in a more animated voice she went on, "But, Caroline, I can't *think* why they should be so keen to get a hold of that book— it's not as if it's possible to hide heaps of diamonds between the leaves of a book."

Vanessa turned away in despair, and Caroline, looking at the distant, snow-topped peaks as Major Morris sped along the lake-side, mused in a dreamy voice, "I once saw a film about spies and things and some secret papers were hidden in a space hollowed out in the leaves of a book. Was there a space hollowed out in *Tales of Mystery,* Sara?"

"Gosh, *no*! I read half the book, I keep telling you," said Sara.

"What about the other half?" asked Caroline.

"D'you think I'm blind, or nuts?" demanded Sara.

"Yes, I do, sometimes," murmured Caroline.

"Well, I'm not so blind as not to notice if there was a great big hole in the middle of a book I'm reading," said Sara affronted, "though as a matter of fact," she went on, "*I* once read a story where a thief hid a pearl necklace behind the spine

of a book—but that was a Bible, I've just remembered. And it was a silly story, anyway." They
both relapsed into thought and John drove on.

So fast and so hard did he drive that outside
Rottweil, a delicious small town whose red roofs
were clustered round the top of a little tree-clad hill,
they had to stop for a while for Sara, who
suddenly announced she was going to be sick, to
recover.

"You'll kill the child," fretted Vanessa, "with
this mad rushing. Can't we stop here for the
night?"

"No, I think we ought to get as far as Baden,"
John replied, and suggested various remedies, most
of them drastic, for Sara; and Sara lay on her back
by the side of the road, and kept insisting that she
was often sick, as they ought to know, that she
knew exactly the course her indisposition would
take, and that she'd be all right in a minute.

"Does your head ache, Sara?" Vanessa asked.

Sara admitted it did, a bit.

"Oh, dear!" said Vanessa. "What's the good
of finding a lot of diamonds—if there are any
diamonds, which I very much doubt—if we're going
to have Sara ill?"

John and Caroline, looking a little worried,
Vanessa was glad to note, admitted the truth of this.

"But," John added, "it would be a queer thing if
a wallop on the head, sufficient to knock her out,
didn't give her a bit of a headache next day.
Probably—"

Sara interrupted him at this point by making a
hurried retreat behind some bushes. A little later

she reappeared and announced that she was perfectly all right, and ready to go on. Vanessa
agreed on condition that she drove, and Sara sat in
front beside her.

"Well, if you want another invalid on your
hands—" said John: "you know what sitting
in the back does to me. Why don't you go in the
back seat?"

"Because you're driving too fast, and it won't
do you a bit of harm to have a taste of your own
medicine," Vanessa told him.

So John reluctantly pushed his way in among
the climbing boots, rugs, the bread-board, coats,
maps, and Caroline, and grumbled quietly all the
way to Baden-Baden.

"You're not thinking of stopping at that frightful *Gasthaus* full of livestock, again, are you?"
Caroline wanted to know, as they were nearing the
town.

"You didn't like it?" John said in an amazed
voice. "You have such conventional ideas, you
two."

"There was a nice little place somewhere this
side of Baden, I noticed," said Vanessa. "It had a
lovely view of the Forest, I should think, but I
don't know if it was one mile or twenty out of the
town."

"As it is now almost dark, the view won't be a
great clue," said John. "Now, if you could only
concentrate—"

Vanessa ignored him, for she had spotted a little
inn. It might or it might not be the one she was
thinking of, but its position looked about right, and

in any case she was determined to go not a wheel's turn farther, because Sara hadn't uttered a word for the past hour, and she wasn't asleep, and this was such an unprecedented state of affairs that Vanessa was convinced that she was concussed or unconscious.

"This looks as if it might be the place," she said in her usual dithery way, "and yet was it called—?"

"This will do, anyway," said Caroline.

They were all thankful to stop, for it had been a tiring day to come after the excitements of the previous night. John got out to interview the landlord.

"Sara, darling, how do you feel?" Vanessa turned anxiously to her.

Sara lifted a languid hand to her head. "I feel awful," she said.

Vanessa was worried. "Have you a pain in your head, or—"

"I don't know exactly," said Sara in a faint voice.

"Oh, dear!" said Vanessa, but Caroline said briskly, gathering up coats and things:

"Well, you'd better hop out of the car and get to bed."

Sara sighed gently at this harshness, and said even more faintly, "I'm *so* sorry to be such a nuisance to you all, but I'm afraid you'll have to carry me."

"Oh, *dear*!" said Vanessa, but fortunately Caroline had had previous experience of Sara in one of her interesting invalid phases, so she leant over the back of the seat and whispered:

"It's absolutely rotten for you to feel so bad, shrimp, but you know if you're terribly ill John'll fetch some horrible German doctor to you and probably leave you behind when we go after the diamonds."

Sara sat up pretty quickly. "Oh, gosh, Caroline, he couldn't be such a brute!" Then, remembering, she said bravely, "I'll try and walk—but I feel awful."

By the time she had had her cut dressed (and, at her own instigation, re-bandaged) and had sunk deep into the softness of another clean luxurious German bed, Sara was beginning to feel rather less awful, and by morning was completely restored to normal. But whereas on Saturday everything had gone off according to plan, except for Sara's little indisposition, Sunday's journey was to prove a different matter entirely.

It began well enough at eight o'clock on a brilliantly sunshiny morning. Vanessa was dragged away unwillingly from the view; John strapped on the luggage with his customary short outburst of bad temper over the operation; Sara was herself again. As they filed in, Sara, who was always helpful at inopportune moments, said:

"What about petrol, John?" And John, fresh from his wrestling match with the haversacks, barked at her:

"Good heavens, girl, d'you think that petrol pumps grow in the middle of nowhere? Do you see any possible means of obtaining petrol in this place?"

"No," Sara admitted, sorry she had brought the subject up, "I just thought I'd mention it."

"Well, mention it when we come to a petrol station. I'm as anxious to get petrol as you are, for we're running low, but it's no good going on about it when we're not near a garage."

Sara was just about to point out that she, personally, wasn't at all anxious to get petrol, and that just to let fall the one word petrol could hardly be called going on about it, but Caroline drew her into the car and whispered:

"Sh!—don't you know *yet* not to speak to John when he's in a wax?"

"Horrid creature," growled Sara, but very quietly, "he's always in a wax." Caroline laughed and said in a low voice, "He doesn't mean a thing —nobody takes his waxes seriously."

"Gosh, I'm glad he's not my brother-in-law!" Sara was still a little put out.

"You'd be a changed girl if I were," came from the driving seat.

"Goodness," said Vanessa, "are you going to squabble *all* this nice May morning?"

"I'm not squabbling," said John, "are you, Sara?"

"Me?" said Sara. "Gosh, who started it, I'd like to know?"

"We're the best of friends, aren't we, Sara?" said John. "Just make sure the luggage is all right, to prove it, and pass me over my hat, there's a good girl.

Sara, feeling she had had the worst of that encounter, banged crossly round to peer at the luggage, and then began the usual scrabble on the floor, on the seat, under rugs, in the rack. Finally she said:

"It's not here, your hat."

"Nonsense!" said John. "It must be there. You have a look, Caroline."

"I have," said Caroline wearily, bored with the hat question. "It's not here."

"Now maybe we'll get peace," murmured Sara.

"Peace?" shouted John, braking so suddenly that they all pitched forward, to their annoyance. "Not on your life," he said, as he proceeded to turn the car. "We're going back for it."

"Oh, *John,*" wailed Sara, "we haven't *time* for this sort of thing—Slippery Sam will get there first and we'll lose the diamonds! Fancy giving up a necklace of priceless diamonds for the sake of that awful old hat."

"Fancy," John answered imperturbably as he drove back to the inn, "giving up a necklace of priceless diamonds for a glass of lemonade."

That silenced Sara completely, but Caroline said to comfort her, "You might as well keep cool, Sara. For one thing old Slippery doesn't know where we, or the diamonds, are, and for another, John wouldn't lose that hat for anything."

"No, indeed," John agreed. "I'd much sooner lose you, Sara."

As they came to the top of the little rise on which the *Gasthof* stood, and turned into the courtyard, a grey car whizzed by, going hard in the direction of Baden-Baden.

K

"Gosh!" yelled Sara, "that was the, Burton-Wares!"

There was an uproar in Major Morris.

John nearly broke his neck as he thrust his head out of the window—to see nothing but a cloud of dust disappearing down the hill. Every one talked at once.

"It *couldn't* have been, Sara!" said Caroline.

"It *was,*" said Sara. "I saw the number."

"Keep in the car, anyway," said John. "They mustn't see us."

"Oh, dear!" moaned Vanessa.

"What are they doing here?" exclaimed Caroline.

"They're after us, of course—"

"Are you *sure,* Sara—?"

"Of course I'm sure—I *always* look at numbers, ever since years ago we used to play that game."

"But how do they know we're *here*?"

"Surely, surely," Caroline even hesitated to put the dreadful thought into words, "surely Fritz wouldn't give us away?" she finished all in a rush.

"Oh, dear!" said Vanessa.

"Of course not," said Sara scornfully. "But," she added as a dreadful thought struck her, "maybe they threatened him—with a gun!"

"There would be nothing to stop him telling the story we'd made up, even if threatened," said John. "The point is, they're here—and there seems to be no reason why they should be, except that *we're* here. I'll drive the car behind the inn well out of sight of the road until we talk this over."

The others gabbled on.

"Why didn't they see *us?*" said Sara.

"Well, we were going the opposite way from what they'd expect, for one thing—but in any case we had turned into the inn before they topped the rise, and we would be half hidden," Caroline suggested. "But how did they know we were near Baden?"

"Well," John worked it out, "what would they do? Suppose Fritz told them our story—that we'd gone up the Jungfraujoch. We had a start, but theirs was the faster car; if they went up after us they knew they'd have time to get to Lauterbrunnen, see if our car was there, and wait for us to come down——"

"They'd have to go back to Grindel for their luggage and to pay their hotel bill," interrupted Caroline; "that would take time."

"Not a great deal," said John. "Besides, they may have done that before coming down to the Alpenrose, so that whenever we'd handed over the book they could get away."

"Yes," broke in Sara eagerly, "or they still didn't know for sure we weren't on the level—as far as *they* knew, there was nothing to connect them with the robbery that went wrong at Alpenrose. They'd hope we'd just hand over the book-and even if we did suspect something, as they seem to think we did, we could hardly refuse to give Nasty Nellie her own book——"

"Yes," John swept on, "when they got to Lauterbrunnen, no sign of us, of course. *Now,* what do they do?"

"They might get suspicious *then* that Fritz had spun them a yarn," suggested Caroline.

"And that, added to the suspicions their guilty consciences had given them already," said Sara virtuously, "would give them a nasty jar, because—"

"Got it," yelled John, slapping his hand on the steering wheel: "the garage-man!"

"Garage-man?" said Sara. "What garage-man?"

"The one at Interlaken where we stopped for petrol—I discussed with him the whole route to Baden."

"And I," moaned Caroline, "mentioned Bonn!"

"Oh, gosh!" said Sara. "They've taken a chance when we weren't at Lauterbrunnen, and decided to go to the garages in Interlaken, and of course, got some information at the first one—"

"The man would certainly remember us—it was so early in the morning, things were quiet, and, besides, there are so few G.B. cars about just now," John said.

"And I even told him what good English he spoke," Sara moaned. "Nasty creature, to give us away!"

"Don't be daft, Sara," snorted Caroline; "no earthly reason why he shouldn't."

"Never mind that," said John; "the point is that they may intercept us at any point from here to Rhondorf. And what do we say if they do? That we don't like the look of them, and won't give them back their own book—which, in any case, we haven't got."

"I don't see how we dare risk a meeting," said Caroline, "in case they find out where the book is. We've just got to get to Rhondorf first."

"Gosh, yes!" said Sara, her impish little face screwed up in an expression of grim determination.

"Step on the gas, John, and race them to it."

"That's impossible," said John impatiently; "we haven't got the speed. Give me the map, Vanessa, and we'll see about another road." Vanessa handed over the map as if washing her hands of all responsibility. John spread it out, and Caroline and Sara hung over the back of his seat.

"What a blow we didn't take the Ulm-Stuttgart route from Lake Constance," said Sara; "then we should have missed them."

"It's a colossal stroke of luck we didn't, my girl," John contradicted her. "Now we're on our guard. I wonder what they'll do?—they don't know where we're staying the night, but they know pretty well what the Major's capable of in the way of speed, and they'll deduce we'd get as far as Baden. I'll bet they imagine they're on the road before us this morning, and if I were in their place, looking for someone who's supposed to be in Baden, I'd stop on the other side of the town, on the main road to Karlsruhe and wait there for an hour or two: if they miss us, they know they've enough speed to make up on us before very long."

"So what do we do?" said Sara, breathing heavily down John's neck.

"We'll circle round to Pforzheim, through

Heilbronn, up to Frankfurt, and so to Koblenz: the others will go Heidelberg—Darmstadt, the way we came, what we decided at Interlaken—the man *may* have remembered some of the names we mentioned."

"And at Koblenz?" said Vanessa in a faint voice.

"Then we'll just have to take our chance and keep on the look-out for them—for we can't possibly guess which side of the Rhine they'll take."

Vanessa looked slightly ill, and wondered to herself how she was going to explain to her mother or Aunt Margaret if either Caroline or Sara went home riddled with bullets from the gun of Nasty Nessie taking pot shots at them from behind any tree they might come to. But when she mentioned this the others looked amazed at her timidity, and in shocked tones Caroline put it down to funk.

"Besides," said John, who, Vanessa thought rather crossly, should have had more sense than to encourage the girls, "we don't know if they have guns. And our great safeguard is that they still don't know that we're anything but the most unsuspecting crew of people."

"Well," said Caroline impatiently, "why bother about all that? Let's get going."

John handed the map over to Caroline, with instructions to keep him right.

"I say," said she: "that A.A. route included Stuttgart and Heilbronn. Fish it out, Sara—it might be jolly useful at this point."

John had started the engine when Vanessa said coldly, "Don't you think you might as well get the hat you came back for?" John agreed with enthusiasm, and went in to collect his hat and spin some yarn to explain their lurking about the courtyard to the innkeeper's wife, who had been taking surreptitious glances at them through the window for some time.

"*Dear* hat!" said Sara. "But for that hat old Slippery would have made up on us, and at this moment we'd have been in a spot. And I say, don't you think we ought to disguise the car in some way, in case they come on us unexpectedly?"

"How?" said Caroline.

They got out to inspect.

"The G.B. plate and the number plates are pretty well disguised already," said Caroline, "with the dust."

"What about the luggage?" said Sara.

It was indeed a sorry sight. Leaving the Alpenrose, the girls had had some qualms at the condition of Sara's poor father's beautiful hogskin bag, all stained and discoloured with dirt; so, in a panic, they had decided to wrap newspaper round it each morning. So newspaper, tossed and torn by the wind, festooned the already unsightly pile of soiled bag and haversacks, and Sara was just suggesting that a towel wrapped round and hanging down would obscure the number plate better when John emerged, and ordered them back into the car in a hurry.

"Now, off we go," he said—growing more like a child every minute, thought Vanessa disgustedly, "and keep your eyes skinned, you two at the back, in case they, too, double back on their tracks. You take the A.A. route, Vanessa, and see if it's any good for us," he said, edging the car on to the main road.

Vanessa meekly took the by now rather battered route from Sara, and sighed as she thought of the peaceful law-abiding holiday she had visualised when first she scanned it.

CHAPTER FOURTEEN

Two miles out of Pforzheim Major Morris hiccoughed once or twice and came slowly to a standstill. Vanessa looked up from her A.A. route, Sara and Caroline turned round from glueing their noses to the rear-window as they kept watch for Slippery Sam and Nasty Nellie through the haze of dust raised by the Major's progress.

"What is it?" said Sara fearfully.

John turned a rueful face towards them and said, "No petrol! In the excitement, I quite forgot we were running short."

"Thank goodness it's no worse!" Vanessa breathed. "And perhaps the walk on to—what's the next place? Pforzheim? Like a sneeze—will calm you down a little, and you'll realise that all this is madness, absolute madness."

"But, darling," said John, "I don't think it would be at all wise for me to walk to Pforzheim and leave the car, and yourselves, unprotected—"

"I'll go," interrupted Sara. "I'll go for petrol;

you come with me, Caro, and John can stay here to guard the car, just in case. Gosh, how I wish you had a gun, John!" Vanessa thanked goodness that he hadn't, and John, who, although he did feel he should stay by the car, also felt for Sara's and Caroline's trudge, said doubtfully:

"What about the language question—you won't find every one talking English here, as in Switzerland."

"Oh, gosh," said Sara, "we can surely get some *petrol* in German!"

Caroline, all the same, took the precaution of putting her dictionary and her *All you want to know in Germany* in her pocket, collected some money from John, and philosophically if not enthusiastically, set off with Sara.

"This should be easy," said that optimist, as they hurried along. But, as Caroline had noticed before in a foreign country, it was the apparently easy things which proved full of unexpected difficulties. To begin with, they couldn't find a garage. They searched up and down likely-looking streets, they inquired, and followed, as they thought, the directions given, but never a garage appeared.

"Gosh," said Sara crossly, "you'd think they were trying to hide the things!"

"Garages are always at the other end of a town from where you are if you want one," said Caroline.

"And if you don't you're always tripping over them. Let's walk right along the main street—we're bound to come to one eventually."

"Yes, but it's all wasting *time,*" fumed Sara.

"Keep calm. I expect Sam and Nellie are at

Heidelberg by now. I say, there's a hotel, quite a decent-sized one: they're sure to have a garage attached—come over and we'll see."

They seemed to be in luck at last; there was a garage, and there was a pleasant man in attendance, and Sara began to tell him what they wanted. When she had finished, he looked quite, quite vacant.

"Tut!" said Sara, disappointed. "I thought that was *very* clear. Oh, well, here goes again!" But Caroline was taking no chances: she ruffled the pages of her phrase book, found what she wanted and firmly pointed with her finger to what she considered the politest request for petrol. After a few puzzled seconds a great light seemed to break on the pleasant man, and, beaming, he hurried across the garage, followed by Sara and Caroline, opened a sliding door—and they found that they were being proudly presented with a lock-up.

"Oh, no, no!" said Caroline, when she realised this was all they were getting. "*Benzin, Benzin!*" But the man, as if offended they hadn't taken his beautiful lock-up, just shook his head, and kept on shaking it.

"This is hopeless," said Caroline. "Besides, I don't see any petrol-pumps anyway. Come on." So with a *"Danke schön"* they went out into the streets again. About a hundred yards farther on, the familiar shapes of petrol-pumps loomed into view, and they hurried towards them as eagerly as if they held all the beauty of the Alps and more.

"Thank goodness!" said Sara. "The *time* we're wasting." The petrol was there and the attendant was there—this time a tidy-looking woman—and when they had asked for petrol, she smiled and nodded, but said, in a slightly puzzled voice:

"Where is the auto?"

"What on earth does it matter to her *where* the auto is?" said Sara, exasperated, in a low voice; however, they indicated vaguely the way they had come, and explained as best they could just where the auto was situated. She looked at them as if they were to be pitied rather than blamed, pointed down the road, pointed to the petrol-pumps, gabbled something, shrugged, and smiled.

It took time and a lot of patience on Caroline's part (and a lot of jumping about, making exasperated noises on Sara's) to get the woman to see what they were driving at, but she succeeded ultimately: a can, rather battered, was filled, Caroline vowed—or thought she did—to bring it back, and with Sara hopping, skipping, and jumping at her side to keep up with her, they set off. Half a mile out of the town they were astounded to see Major Morris come spanking along to meet them.

"You needn't have bothered to go," John grinned at them, through the window: "a passing car gave me enough to get into Pforzheim."

"For two pins I'd hit you over the head with this can," said Caroline. "You don't know what we've been through." John didn't ask for details—he didn't have to, for Sara was recounting them, with suitable embellishments, to Vanessa.

John laughed as he climbed out of the car. "I may as well put your contribution into the tank," he said. "It'll all help."

He was screwing on the cap of the tank when a car, travelling very fast in the direction of Pforzheim, swished past, and in a whirl of dust and with a grinding of brakes drew up about twenty yards beyond them.

"Oh, gosh," said Sara, "it's them!"

"It's they," said Vanessa, but without conviction.

"Now, listen," said John rapidly, as they watched two figures descend from the car in front, "act absolutely naturally—heaven knows *what* may depend on it—Vanessa, you dither at the woman—you two keep your heads, and *don't give yourselves away.*"

The man approached, peeling a pair of goggles from his eyes, followed by the woman in a white coat and helmet and sun-glasses, saying as he came in a harsh voice, "Can I be of any assistance?"— then giving a beautifully simulated start of surprise, he said, "Why, it's *you*! Darling," turning to his wife, "it's Sara and Caroline Storm—and—?" and he stopped and waited expectantly.

"This is my sister, Mrs. Douglas," mumbled Caroline, "and her husband—Mr. and Mrs. Burton-Ware. You know, Vanessa, we told you about meeting Mr. and Mrs. Burton-Ware in Grindelwald."

"How *do* you do?" gushed Mrs. Burton-Ware. "What an *extraordinary* coincidence—"

"Of course I remember, Caroline," said Vanessa. "How do you do? Nasty—nasty, nasty time we've been having," she fluttered, recovering herself. "Ran out of petrol, you know."

"Agony for you," said Mrs. Burton-Ware, "but of course we can give you some, can't we, darling? But what *fun* meeting you here! And now," she giggled archly, turning to Sara, "you'll be able to give me my book."

"Oh," said Sara, "your book. But—but I—I sent it to England," and she smiled, very pleased with herself. For the first time the Burton-Wares betrayed themselves. There was a deathly silence; the mask of geniality slipped, and for an instant a look of sheer hate, so swift that it had gone almost before it could be registered, came into the man's eyes as he looked at Sara.

"Oh, gosh, yes," Sara hurried on, crossing her fingers into the most complicated shapes behind her back, "didn't you get my message? When we decided to leave Grindelwald a little sooner I posted your book to the address on the card you gave us. I do hope I have done the right thing?" she finished earnestly.

"Yes, rather, that was sweet of you. My maid is in the flat in London." Nellie was herself again. "And where are you going now?" she turned to Vanessa.

"Where are we going? Do *you* ever know where you're going in a car?" Vanessa rambled, as instructed. "That's what I find so fascinating about this type of holiday. Never know in the morning where you'll be in the evening—Berlin, Hamburg—there are so many marvellous places—but, of course, we must be in Calais on Wednesday, for we've booked our place in the Townsend Ferry for that day—we shall all be desperately sorry to go home—"

"About that petrol you so kindly offered, Mr. —er?" John said, smiling.

"Burton-Ware," supplied Slippery Sam, with perhaps a little too much heartiness. "Of course, I'll get you some—we've been carrying a spare tin always on this trip, as a matter of fact—saves trouble in the long run, eh?"

"May I come and look at your car?" begged Caroline, with her most innocent expression. "She's a beauty, isn't she? Pretty fast, I should think," she said, as the two of them walked towards the Armstrong-Siddeley together. "May I look inside?" she said, as Burton-Ware opened the boot to get out the petrol.

"Do, do," said Burton-Ware.

They went back to the Major with the petrol, and John poured it into his tank.

"It's extraordinary kind of you," he assured Slippery Sam.

"Not at all, not at all," said Sam.

John went on—" And now we must be getting along. Come along you two, and Vanessa," and he bundled them all into Major Morris; and with many expressions of gratitude, and expectations that they would be sure to meet somewhere else on the road, he drove off, while Mr. and Mrs. Burton-Ware, looking so affable, waved them good-bye.

As soon as they were out of all possible earshot, babel broke loose.

"What *filthy* luck! What made them come this way?"

"Because we never turned up at Baden, I suppose they thought they'd try scouting around."

"I'm exhausted, mouthing stupidities at that woman. And I nearly called her Nasty Nessie!"

"Gosh, yes, I wanted to scream!—but *wasn't* that a good story I told her, that I posted her book?"

"Sara," said John, "you were marvellous. Of course—unless that address was bogus, which isn't likely, when all their efforts are spent on looking as like the genuine article as possible—they'll telephone their house to hear of its arrival, and believe me they'll keep a pretty sharp eye on us just the same."

"Won't they be as sick as mud though, either way?" gloated Sara. "If we're as stupid as we seem, and have sent the book to London, I'll bet the last thing they want to do is to go back home and collect it and risk the customs again; or if they have it posted—and the parcel should be examined! They'll be frantic. And if the book *doesn't* arrive, they won't know what to think. And Vanessa, you old sport, impressing on Nellie the day we were going back to England."

"Well," said Vanessa, "somebody had to see that they'd be at Dover to be arrested!"

"Hurrah!" cheered Sara. "Vanessa's seen the light at last."

"But what will they do now?" worried John, "I'm sure they'll stick closer than brothers to us till they know what's happened, but we *must* shake them off until we reach Rhondorf."

"Well, actually," said Caroline, who up till now

had not uttered a word, "we have shaken them off for a bit."

"What do you mean?" said John.

"This," said Caroline, and while Sara boggled, she thrust her fist between John and Vanessa, and opened it. There, on her palm, lay a switch-key.

CHAPTER FIFTEEN

THE rejoicing over the fact that the Burton-Wares were stuck where they were for a while had not ceased by the time they had returned the petrol tin, filled up with petrol, and stopped for a second to buy some food for lunch.

"We'll not be just so popular the next time we meet the Burton-Wares," mused John as they tore on, "so the best thing to do is not meet them. I think we shouldn't make any detour now, but take advantage of this start, go back to the Karlsruhe-Heidelberg road, the way we know (a little, at least), and go as hard as we can for Rhondorf. And," he added, giving a wicked chuckle, "aren't we in for it, if *Tales of Mystery* reveals itself to be nothing but an innocent book?"

"Nonsense!" said Vanessa, while Sara and Caroline listened in amazement to this *volte-face*: "there's something in that book, or that horrible Nessie wouldn't be so anxious about it. Coming up pretending to be good Samaritans, not knowing it was us."

John laughed. "All the same," he said, "sometimes an ordinary nail-file acts as well as a switch-key, and I expect Nellie has a nail-file, all right—"

"I shouldn't think she has, judging by her long red nails," interrupted Caroline.

"The important thing is," went on John, "that we can't afford to relax. Slippery Sam may make up on us any time."

"Can we make Rhondorf to-night?" Sara asked.

"I think so, if we're unmolested," said John. "We did Rhondorf to Baden in one day, and we weren't hurrying, and we didn't leave any too early in the morning. But to do it, we'll have to push on."

They pushed on. Fortunately—as Sara remarked in one of her infrequent intervals from wondering aloud where Sam and Nellie had got to and how on earth that book could be concerned with diamonds —he kept his hat firmly clamped on his head. And equally fortunately either no one felt ill or no one had the courage to mention it, for John never looked like stopping.

They pushed on. Round about Darmstadt Sara began talking in a loud voice about tea, but it led to nothing. She was still talking about it at Mainz, and it was still leading to nothing. So she began talking about dinner instead, and at Koblenz John actually relented so far as to suggest they might stop and have some. "After all," he said, "we haven't heard a squeak of them, and we hadn't much lunch."

Sara agreed. "In fact," she said, "I would

hardly call it lunch, a couple of dry rolls and a
piece of cheese—"

"And two apples and half a pound of chocolate," added Caroline.

"Oh, well," said Sara, "if you count in every
single thing."

They hid the car as best they could up a side
street, and found a little quiet restaurant from which
they could watch the main road. They were all glad
of the rest and a decent meal eaten in reasonable
comfort.

"They might try to pick up our trail here," said
John, as they were finishing. "Although I don't
think they will bother us much until they hear if the
book has reached England. However, we'll certainly watch for 'em. Which bank of the river shall
we take?"

"Left," said Sara, and "Right," said Caroline
simultaneously.

"Which is left, and which right?" Vanessa
murmured.

"We'll toss for it," said John. "Heads for the
Godesberg bank, tails for the Rhondorf one," but
as he tossed with a mark and there followed a discussion as to which *was* heads and which tails, the
whole conversation threatened to keep running
round in vicious circles.

"Does it matter?" said Caroline, bored. "Let's
take the right bank. At least we know the road a
little, and it'll save crossing." As they were preparing to leave the restaurant, Sara began behav-
ing in a most odd manner. She slunk away from
their table, half crouched behind the door, stuck

her head out furtively, and peered up and down the street. Then she turned to the rest of the party, who, along with the other diners in the restaurant, were watching her, and beckoned them. "All clear!" she assured them.

"It's a ghastly feeling, this never knowing when that dreadful couple will pounce on us," shuddered Vanessa. "But I must say Sara doesn't help to ease the tension.

They pushed on. No Burton-Wares leapt out at them from the roadside in the dark; in fact, Sara seemed to be finding the journey so tame that she went to sleep. She awoke to find herself being prodded in the ribs, and she snarled, angrily and sleepily: "You can take that gun off me, you chiseler!" But the chiseler was only Caroline, after all, and the gun was only her sharp forefinger.

"Wake up," she was saying. "We're here."

"Where?" asked Sara vacantly.

"In the Adlerstrasse. John's gone to ask Frau Roedig if she can take us in."

Frau Roedig could. She did not seem unduly surprised, only rather touched and pleased to see them again, gave them, to their gratification, the rooms they had occupied before, and told them she had expected they would come again. John assured her gallantly that they could not resist another visit to the beautiful Rhine and to her so-comfortable house.

"*Ach so!*" she beamed, and went off to fill their hot-water bottles.

The four of them gathered in the girls' room, and John, trying to keep in check his rising excitement, said, "Now, Sara, produce your waiter's name and address, and we'll go and pay him a little visit. He'll hardly be at the top of the Drachenfels at this time of the evening."

"Oh, gosh!" said Sara. "Can you believe that we're here at last, and that in a second we'll have the book and know everything!" She was searching through her diary, her purse, in the corners of her satchel as she spoke.

The others sat and watched, eagerly, silently. "Tut!" she said, knelt on the bed, turned the bag inside out and began again to go through the extraordinary jumble of combs, bits of paper, purse, diary, and pieces of chocolate, which emerged.

"What a mess!" murmured Caroline.

Sara's search, as she began on the pile for the third time, became a little feverish. The tension in the room increased. When she had turned over everything that would turn, and examined every piece of paper, she sat back on her heels, lifted a distraught face, and whispered, "It's not there!"

The tension broke. Vanessa groaned. John looked as if, at any moment, he was about to burst. Caroline breathed—and it was a wish rather than a conviction— "It *must* be!"

"Oh, gosh," said Sara desperately, "it *isn't*! Have a look, Caro."

"Where did you put it?" asked Caroline, beginning on the most likely-looking of the dirty little scraps of paper.

"In my diary, in the pocket thing at the back, I thought. I'm *sure* I put it there."

"You imbecilic little—!" John started, but

Vanessa laid a restraining hand on his arm and said:

"Is there any other place you could have put it, Sara, dear, or do you remember the address?"

Sara was much less able to cope with Vanessa's gentleness than with John's rage. She blinked rapidly once or twice and gulped, then managed to get out, "No. I'm certain I put it there. The waiter—I think his name was Beethoven, because I remember being a bit surprised, for I thought Beethoven was a composer—wrote his name and address on a piece of paper, and I folded it up and put it in there—I *think*—gosh, it's *so* difficult to remember!—but I know I remember thinking I must put it in a safe place."

"Well, you seem to have done that all right," said Caroline grimly. "It's not among this lot. Why do you hoard such useless rubbish, Sara? All those old shop bills. And surely he couldn't be called Beethoven?"

"Well," said Vanessa, "wasn't Beethoven or Bach or someone born about here? This waiter is probably called after the local celebrity."

"And now," John, who had been foaming quietly at the mouth in a corner, could contain himself no longer, "perhaps when you have finished these musical reminiscences you will all tell me what we are going to do? And just bear in mind that we've come half-way across Europe to collect this book; we've behaved shockingly to a couple of apparently law-abiding citizens on holiday—the only justification for such behaviour being the discovery of something criminal connected with the book. And now we can't even *get* the book. And why? Because Sara is such a—"

"Oh, John," interrupted Caroline wearily, "save your breath! We all—including Sara, I should think by this time—know that Sara has a brain like a sieve: why go on about it? Calm down, and think of something we can *do.*"

"The only thing I can think of," said John, grinning unwillingly at Caroline and her bossiness, "is to exterminate Sara."

"That wouldn't help," murmured Vannessa, "would it?"

"It would help me considerably," said John, "but before I start on you, Sara, you'd better go up the Drachenfels to find Beethoven and extract the book from him."

"What, now?" Sara asked in alarm.

"Oh, someone else talk to her," John burst out again. "She's driving me mad—"

"There is just one thing which doesn't seem to have occurred to any of you," Caroline's cool voice broke in. "We're all calmly expecting to find the book just as Sara left it. But suppose old Beethoven has discovered the secret, and is away blueing the proceeds somewhere?"

"Oh, dear," sighed Vanessa, "this party's getting sadder and sadder! I wonder how many years you get for stealing switch-keys?"

"Gosh!" said Sara, rather annoyed. "He couldn't possibly discover something I missed."

"You think not?" murmured John nastily, but he added, "No, I think we're safe enough from Beethoven's prying eyes: to begin with, he pro-

bably hasn't opened the book, but just wanted to
possess a handsome English book, or if he has I
should think the secret is pretty well concealed.
And if he had found anything he'd be run in whenever he tried to raise money on it, because the
description of that necklace will be over Europe as
well as Britain by now. And if that's happened,"
he added, looking thoughtfully at Sara, "the
police will be waiting for you, Sara, to come back
and collect your swag."

"Oh, gosh!" said Sara.

"And you certainly haven't much of a story—
saying you found the book in the car," John was
going on, while Sara's green eyes widened, "and
I doubt—yes, I doubt very much—if the Burton-
Wares will come forward to corroborate your story.
You can think over *that* for the rest of the evening.
Come along, Vanessa—I feel a little stroll would
refresh me wonderfully before bed."

"Looks as though John's off you at the
moment," Caroline remarked, as the door closed
behind the Douglases. Besides this new occasion
for nervousness, Sara was suffering all the discom-
fort of knowing she was in the wrong, and so she
tried to brazen it out.

"Well, gosh," she blustered, "I'm off him!
You'd think I'd thrown the beastly paper away!"

"I expect you did," said Caroline.

"And Caroline—do *you* think the police will be
waiting to nab me as soon as I start inquiring for
the book?"

Caroline considered for a moment. "No," she
said finally, "I don't. For one thing, every one

would know by this time, Frau Roedig would have been certain to hear about it, and I'm sure she wouldn't have given us such a welcome if she had thought we were thieves. Or, at least," she added, "she'd have given us a different kind of welcome."

"Oh, gosh, I hope so! But maybe she is a very good actor, and she has gone to fetch the police," sighed Sara, peering out through a chink in the curtains as if expecting to see a detachment of police come marching up the street to arrest her. "If only I hadn't lost that address we would know every-thing, and there wouldn't be this awful suspense. It's ghastly, really, now we can't put our hands on it, whatever has happened—whether there's a clue in it to the diamonds, or whether Beethoven's found the clue, told the police how he got it, and we get thrown into prison."

"Only you, shrimp. The rest of us know nothing about it," Caroline grinned at her. "But do stop moaning over spilt milk—we'll show John a thing or two yet. Bed now for you, my girl—"

"I shan't sleep a wink—"

"Well, you must go just the same, so that you can get up really bright and early for your ascent to-morrow."

"Aren't you—" Sara began, but stopped, and sighed, and said no more. And in a gloomy, dis-couraged silence the two went to bed.

They rose at a grey hour on a grey morning. Caroline awoke reluctantly at six to find Sara half-dressed and banging clumsily about in semi-obscurity.

"Why are we in darkness?" Caroline growled, rolling out of bed.

"Well, I didn't want to disturb you," Sara, very chastened of mood this morning, assured her earnestly.

"That was bright of you. Did you think I was going to climb up the Drachenfels in my pyjamas and sound asleep?"

Sara looked at her, pleased and surprised. "But are you—I didn't think you were—gosh, Caroline, goody-goody!" she stammered. Caroline lifted one eyebrow at her, grinned, and went on washing.

They crept down Frau Roedig's stairs and cautiously unbolted Frau Roedig's door. Then they crept upstairs again—to collect mackintoshes, for it was pouring with rain.

"Isn't this agony!" sighed Caroline, tying a waterproof hood over her pale gold hair.

"Oh, a walk in the rain's rather nice!" Sara maintained bravely. "And the trees will shelter us."

"Not when it starts going down your neck," Caroline answered gloomily.

It started to do that about half-way up, for the trees, heavy with rain, were inclined to prove the reverse of sheltering, tipping their burden of water on to the girls as they passed. Caroline tied a handkerchief round her neck and squelched gloomily on. Sara's ardour for walking in the rain had been quenched some time before, but her passion for speech remained, and she kept up for the benefit of an unheeding, unsympathetic world a running commentary dealing with martyrdom and misery:

"Never make up for this wetness, even if I hang with diamonds. Thank goodness," she finished up, "this is about the top. I don't suppose the *biergarten's* open at this time, but the waiters will be about somewhere, I expect."

But there was not a human being to be seen, and the *biergarten*—all the little iron chairs cocked up on top of the tables—was not only closed but looked as if it would be that way for days and days.

"For a week, in fact," said Caroline furiously, peering through the locked glass doors of the restaurant building. "I bet you what you like that so early in the season it only opens at week-ends. What fools we were not to ask Frau Roedig where to find Beethoven! In a tiny village like Rhondorf every one's bound to know every one else."

"Gosh, yes," groaned Sara, "how utterly stupid of us! It must have been all that motoring that deadened our wits. Quick, back—before John thinks of it," and they took to their heels and went clumping heavily down the path again in their wet shoes.

"It's a great pity," panted Caroline, "that we had to climb away up here before we had this idea" —but Sara had nothing to say to this because at that moment the speed of her downward progress became too much for her equilibrium, which she lost, and she went rolling down the hill.

So they were a sorry sight, soaking wet and bedraggled, and, in Sara's case more or less covered with mud, when they presented themselves at Frau Roedig's kitchen door.

"Now, I'll do the talking," said Caroline, "or

we'll find we're talking about her knitting or her baby or something." It took a little time to convince Frau Roedig, shocked at first at their appearance, that they weren't asking for a supply of hot water and towels. Next she insisted on repeatedly gabbling something at them, the only words of which they could distinguish being *Kurhaus— Fruhstuck—Schwester.*

"What's she saying?" muttered Sara. "Have you got the address yet?"

"She says, I *think,* that our sister is having breakfast at the Kurhaus, and, goodness, we haven't got to the address business yet." But Caroline was game and patient, and, though her German was practically non-existent, she managed to say very firmly in a mixture of that language and broad Scots, "Do you know where a waiter at the Drachenfels beer-garden lives—his name is Beethoven?" This gave rise, Caroline always maintained, to a dissertation on *the* Beethoven and his birthplace at Bonn, but she worked the conversation back to Rhondorf and *its* holder of the illustrious name, and finally she was able to report, aside to Sara, "Hurrah! He lives with his mother in the next street—6 Bergstrasse—name's Beethoven Schmidt—Frau Roedig doesn't think much of him—*Bitte, meine Frau?*—I can't get this bit—*Bitte?* Ah, so! —he got the sack the other day —because he was always reading books!"

"Come *on,*" cried Sara then in a fever. So Caroline only stopped to say, "*Danke schön,*" and they dashed out again.

"Always reading books!" Sara muttered as they ran, "Oh, gosh!"

"If he got the sack from the Drachenfels he might be anywhere by now," Caroline reminded her.

"Don't," said Sara. "I couldn't bear it."

She didn't have to. Number 6 Bergstrasse was a charming little black-and-white cottage neat as a new pin, and the door was opened in reply to their knock by Herr Beethoven Schmidt himself.

"Oh, thank *goodness*!" Sara nearly sobbed.

"You do the talking this time," Caroline muttered.

"That's easy—he speaks English," Sara answered out of the side of her mouth—and began.

Beethoven Schmidt was pleased enough to see her again, to think that she had taken the trouble to call and ask how his studies were progressing, as she declared, but when she edged round to the return of *Tales of Mystery* his thin, eager face fell.

"Ach, but it is the wonderfully beautiful book!" he said. "I treasure that book."

"Yes, I'm sure you do," Sara agreed, "but look, I have brought you enough money—give me some marks, Caroline, quick—to buy many wonderfully beautiful books," and she held invitingly up the twenty mark note produced by Caroline. Beethoven cheered up a bit at the sight of it, and finally went off to fetch *Tales of Mystery*.

"Hope we haven't given him too much, and he suspects something," worried Caroline. "Twenty marks is a lot to pay for a glass of lemonade."

"Oh, it'll be all right," said Sara; "he'll never

think," and she hopped from one foot to another, and when Beethoven came back and handed over the book, she was so excited and her hands trembled so much that she dropped it in the mud; but fortunately Beethoven, a careful soul, had it well covered with newspaper, so it came to no harm.

"*Danke, danke schön!*" breathed Sara fervently when she had it safely in her hands, and "*Danke, danke schön!*" bowed Beethoven, casting a happy glance at his twenty-mark note.

"Now, now, *now*," Sara was rapidly becoming incoherent. We'll find the diamonds and tear it to bits—"

"Steady on," said Caroline. "I'm hungry and I'm wet. I vote we hide it somewhere in our room, get into dry clothes, have some breakfast, and then we'll tell the others and look into it all together." Sara was appalled at this cold-bloodedness, but Caroline managed to persuade her, and they changed, and ran over to the Kurhaus to join Vanessa and John.

Sara did her best not to let them suspect anything, but half-way through, Vanessa, who had been glancing every now and then at her bright eyes and red cheeks, leant over and laid a cool hand on her forehead.

"Have you got a fever, Sara, dear?" she asked.

"No, she's just her usual dotty self," John said, pointing to Sara's roll which she had been plastering with both jam and honey. "Quite right, Sara," he added: "you stoke up. You'll need sustenance for your long trek up the Drachenfels." Sara grinned slyly at Caroline and, to John's surprise, couldn't control a nervous giggle. "Nor is it a very nice morning for your walk," he added nastily. At this Sara guffawed and said:

"Caroline, I can't keep it in any longer—I must tell them." She stopped, looked around to ensure she had their full attention, and announced, "We've got the book."

Vanessa stopped in the act of lifting a cup of coffee to her mouth; John let his knife fall with a clatter on his plate.

"Good gracious!" he exclaimed. "Then what on earth are we all sitting here for? Come along! Where is it?" He rose, Vanessa and Sara with him; their exit was almost a stampede.

"I'm hungry," grumbled Caroline, but as for once no one was paying any attention, she grabbed a roll and followed after them.

When they reached their bedroom Sara had already pulled the book out from under the mattress, and was clawing with feverish hands at its wrapping of newspaper.

"Now," she said, when she had bared it. It was certainly a handsome book, larger than an ordinary novel, and thick. It was new, and the binding was a rich, but unobtrusive brown leather.

"Very handsome," said John. "Well, go on, Sara, open it." Sara was sitting on her bed holding the book in her lap and staring at it. She raised her eyes and almost whispered:

"I don't think I dare."

John made an exasperated noise and bent over to take the book, but that was not what Sara meant at all. Moving it quickly out of his reach she opened it. Whether she expected some strange metamorphosis to have taken place since last she laid eyes on the title-page, whether she expected now to find the pages encrusted with diamonds isn't certain, but anyway it hadn't and they weren't. The title-page revealed nothing more sensational than the name of the book, its author and publisher. She turned the pages over rapidly, while the others watched, goggle-eyed, but the more she turned, the more ordinary they seemed to become; she turned to the back, she turned to the front, she put it to her ear and rattled it, she poked it and prodded it; finally she lifted it by its two covers and shook it. Not a diamond fell out. So she flung it down on the bed and glowered at it. John seized it, and, although a little more roughly, went through much the same process; then Caroline got it, and, in her thorough way, scrutinised it from the most unlikely angles, sounded it, and examined every page. At last she too laid it down gently and said, "Looks like we've made a slight mistake."

Vanessa shut her eyes, and to her unwilling mind was conjured up a picture of the Burton-Wares, on a road between Baden-Baden and Pforzheim, walking over to their grey Armstrong-Siddeley—and finding that there they were stranded, their switch-key gone. She groaned. Sara was thinking "Oh, gosh, sold again! It seems I'm never, *never* going to have the luck to come up against some real crooks." John said to himself, "Well, I shouldn't have listened to them; and now we have messed up a perfectly good tour, and it's doubtful if we'll even get home without a lot more unpleasantness if we meet the Burton-Wares again." Caroline was wondering if the switch-key business would mean prison or Borstal. Suddenly, Vanessa opened her eyes, grabbed the book, and, to every one's horror, began tearing it up.

"Oh, gosh, John," cried Sara, "stop her, quick, she's gone crazy!"

"John, get that book," said Caroline. "It'll be bad enough explaining to the Burton-Wares as it is—what'll it be like if we've to send back a book that's all torn?"

Vanessa looked up from her fell work and grinned. "Don't be silly, Caroline, darling," she enjoined, "I'm not tearing it *all* up. It just suddenly struck me that, even for a leather-bound book, the covers are extraordinarily thick, so I am just having a look at the binding." She tore off the front end-papers, and, instead of boards, revealed a surface that looked like metal.

"Hallo!" exclaimed John, as they all crowded round.

"Have you found something?" Sara's voice was scarcely above a whisper. Caroline swallowed twice and opened her mouth, but no sound came. Vanessa tapped, and pressed and pushed, and as she did so a panel of the metal slid upwards under her hand, and in the oblong space revealed was white cotton-wool.

"Lift it, Sara," said Vanessa. "Gently, though!" Sara, trembling, lifted the almost wafer-thin pad of cotton-wool, and there, on their white bed, glistening and sparking many-coloured fire as the light caught them, pure as great drops of water, lay the Phillimore diamonds.

CHAPTER SIXTEEN

"HONESTLY, is that them?" Sara asked for the fiftieth time.

"Well," said John, in high good-humour, now that all their misdemeanours and discomforts had been justified, but getting a little bored with Sara's parrot-like and ungrammatical question, "they look like diamonds, don't they? What's the trouble?"

"Well," said Sara. It would break her heart now to find there had been any mistake, but she just had to be *sure*. "The papers said it was a diamond *necklace* which had been stolen, not a lot of loose diamonds."

"Dear, dear, Sara! And you the expert in the party! Don't you know that all good jewel thieves take the stones out of their setting, or have them taken, before they smuggle them out of the country to be sold?"

"Of course," beamed Sara, relieved. "It's more murders I have been going in for lately than jewel robberies, so I forgot. Gosh, isn't this a thrill! Fancy us putting it across a jewel thief, and capturing the loot! Fancy us doing old Slippery Sam in the eye!"

M

"Well, I don't know if you could say we had exactly done him in the eye—yet," expostulated Caroline.

"No, indeed," interrupted John; "we still have to get the stuff to Dover and have our two pals arrested. And it is going to be much more ticklish from now on, because now we know they are criminals, and probably not above biffing us on the head if it suits them—"

"They're not above *that*," Sara agreed fervently.

"And *they* know we don't fancy them, or we wouldn't have put their car out of action; and we're in possession of thousands of pounds worth of diamonds."

"Goodness!" said Vanessa. "Let's forget all about that, go as fast as we can from here to Calais, and when we reach Dover go straight to a police station."

"Simple and direct," said John, "but it won't quite do. We mustn't lose the crooks, whatever happens—what would Scotland Yard say to us, Sara?—but I shouldn't wonder if they'd make for Calais now and wait there: it's the only point they're certain we'll go to—whether on the day we said or not—more probably not, *they'll* expect. What we have to do is get on the Ferry ourselves and entice them on to it without being laid out in the process—"

"Couldn't you telephone Scotland Yard?" said Vanessa.

"They wouldn't believe us," said John.

"Don't you know any one at Scotland Yard,

John," sighed Sara, "that you could get in touch with?"

"There's Tubby——" said Vanessa.

"Yes, but he is a very minor young man at Hendon," John demurred.

"Well, but if you telephoned or telegraphed him," Sara urged, "he could go and convince the C.I.D., and they could send some plain-clothes men to meet us at Dover and arrest Sam and Nellie."

"D'you think *any* of them will believe us?" said John sceptically. "Still, we'll try it, and it would certainly relieve my mind considerably."

So they all trooped off to find a telephone, and there was the excitement of putting through a long-distance call. At long last Tubby's faint voice could be heard crackling and spluttering at the other end, and John, very cautiously but firmly, told his story. The unfortunate Tubby said that if this was John's idea of a joke it was a jolly rotten one, because he, Tubby, was hungry, and John was keeping him from his lunch; but John exercised commendable and unusual patience, finally convinced him, and left Tubby assuring him that he had all the facts and would see what he could do with the Criminal Investigation Department.

"Oh, John," said Sara in an ecstasy, when John rejoined them and gave them the news, "you were in touch with the C.I.D.!"

"Not exactly," John grinned at her, but he might have spared himself the trouble of denying it. Sara's cup was now full, she felt. First crooks, then diamonds, then the C.I.D.—and before she was very much older, she told herself, she, Sara

Storm, would be talking to at least a Detective Inspector, because she'd have to explain her share in the business—how she had given Beethoven Schmidt *Tales of Mystery*—

"Gosh," she said aloud, as she got to this point, "I'll look pretty silly telling the Chief Inspector that I traded the Phillimore diamonds for a glass of lemonade!"

"Well, if you hadn't," Caroline consoled her, "none of this would have happened, for you'd have handed the book over to Nasty Nellie as soon as she asked for it, at Grindelwald, and that would have been that."

"So really," said Sara, delighted, "it was all owing to my cleverness that we got the diamonds!"

"All owing to your what?" asked Caroline.

They left Rhondorf after lunch; and they reached Louvain without incident. There they spent the night; the next evening saw them approaching Calais.

"I'd rather we stayed outside Calais to-night," John said, "and embark to-morrow with as little hanging about as possible. The Ferry sails at two forty-five.'

"There is nothing much in the way of a place to stop at this side of Calais, as far as I remember," said Caroline. "Let's make a detour and find somewhere on the other side. Slippery Sam won't expect us to arrive from that direction if he is lying in wait for us somewhere."

That is what they did; and found Wissent, a tiny summer resort, deserted in this early season, a few miles from Calais on the Le Touquet-Calais road.

There they spent the night—and Sara was probably the only one who hadn't a broken, disturbed sleep and bad dreams....

John looked worried and preoccupied all morning and through an early lunch, and during the short drive to Calais. When they drove on to the quay and stopped, and John was preparing to go and find the A.A. man to see about tickets and things, two figures sauntered up, apparently aimlessly, and while Slippery Sam blocked the window at John's right and leant in, Nasty Nellie opened one of the rear doors and pushed her bulk in beside Sara and Caroline.

"Why, Mrs. Burton-Ware—" began Vanessa gallantly.

"That's enough from you," said Sam, forgetting his cultured accent. "I've got you covered." Indeed, his right hand, half concealing a wicked-looking little automatic, was leaning over the lowered window. Nellie was feeling in the car-pockets. Sara kicked her as hard as she could on the ankle, but when she gave a sharp exclamation of pain and Sam's hand slid the gun round till it pointed towards her, Sara became very, very still.

"Got it!" said Nellie, opened the book quickly, grunted with satisfaction, and got out.

"This in intolerable!" John began to bluster. "How dare you—"

"*Good*-morning!" Mr. Burton-Ware smiled, and he and the woman walked leisurely away, out of sight, up a side street.

John interrupted the clamour of rage and disappointment. "Shut up, all of you!" he said. "Get on to the ferry—Sara, take your musical box, and don't let it out of your sight; and keep beside people, sailors or other passengers, till I come."

Utterly mystified, they did what they were told. Sara, nearly in tears, as she saw her pleasant interview with the C.I.D. disappearing, not to mention the diamonds, took the parcel which was the musical box down from the book-rack.

"What colossal cheek," stormed Caroline, "holding us up in broad daylight with crowds of people about. What's John up to, Vanessa, d'you know?"

"I haven't the faintest idea," said Vanessa, "but I could cry."

They filed sadly on to the little Ferry, and, as John had instructed, went and joined the small crowd of passengers who were watching the cars being slung aboard. There, in a little while, John found them. And, as they would have been surprised to see, if they hadn't been too disconsolate to notice, he was rubbing the side of his nose.

"I'll take your parcel, Sara," he said.

"Ugh, throw it into the sea!" said Sara, handing it over. "What's the use of anything now?"

"Oh, I shouldn't do that," John answered, getting a firm grip on it, "for the you-know-whats are inside."

"What!"

"Oh, John, *darling!*"

"Gosh, you don't mean it? You don't mean we've beaten old Slippery after all? Oh, oh—!"

"'Sh!" said John warningly, but very pleased

with himself all the same. "Yes," he went on, low-voiced, as the girls gathered round. "I changed them over in the hotel this morning, pasted down the flyleaf of the book so that it would look undisturbed at a quick glance—"

"But did you *know* they would attack us?" said Sara, filled with admiration.

"I certainly didn't think they would let us walk quietly on to the boat with the goods," said John.

"And I was worried stiff to know what to do—we couldn't let them just lift the stuff from us, and yet I was a bit nervous what would happen to us if we put up any resistance. So I thought a little bluff might do the trick, because I was sure the dear Burton-Wares had no opinion of our brains and wouldn't be expecting any guile."

"John," said Sara, "I think you're wonderful!" and Vanessa and Caroline, smiling at him, nodded.

"The only thing *I'm* sorry about," said Caroline viciously, "and I'm not holding it against you, John, because I think your effort was colossal—but the only thing I regret is that we've lost that revolting couple and won't see them arrested."

"Have we, by Jove!" said John, nodding towards the gangway. The others swung round: the last car had been loaded, and the gangway was just being drawn in, when two people, a man and a woman, hurried up and came aboard.

"What a break!" breathed Sara. "Coming over to England with us to be nabbed!"

"Um. It's a nuisance in a way," frowned John, "that they've discovered their mistake so soon, for once the C.I.D. had heard our story and seen the diamonds, it wouldn't have taken them long to communicate with the French police; but now this pair will be desperate. However, stick together, and keep with the other passengers as much as possible—then I don't think they dare risk anything. Sara, take the parcel, it won't look so obvious if you have it."

"I hope I am not sea-sick, and have to leave you all, and get into their clutches," said Caroline. "But if I were Slippery Sam——"

"Oh, darling, what a horrid idea!" murmured Vanessa.

"—I shouldn't try anything on the boat—much too exposed. I'd wait until you were on the road, and attack you there."

"But I didn't see their car coming on," objected Sara.

"They'll have some of their gang waiting with a car at Dover," suggested Caroline.

"But by then," gloated Sara, rubbing her hands (while the others held their breath for a second's awful suspense as the precious parcel bobbed perilously near the rail), "by then it will be too late."

Such indeed may have been the plan devised by the Burton-Wares; in any case, nothing was seen of them throughout the short sea-passage, and when the cliffs of Dover became clearer and clearer, and the little Ferry sidled up to the quay, John suddenly said, "Good old Tubby!" and his voice sounded relieved. There, sure enough, on the quay was Tubby, who, as Sara pointed out, wasn't a bit tubby, and with him were two tall unobtrusive-looking men.

"Is it possible," asked Sara, tentatively, as if this were too good to be true, "that these are plain-clothes men?"

It was true enough. John, herding his flock before him, saw to it that they were about first off the boat, and Tubby came to meet him and intro-duced—and it was for Sara one of the major thrills of the whole affair—Chief Inspector McPherson and Detective-Sergeant Coles.

"Hand over the diamonds, Sara," prompted John, for Sara seemed to have gone into a trance, gazing enraptured at the two detectives. And Sara started and blushed and grinned, while John gave a quick account of the latest developments.

"If you could just indicate the couple as they disembark, Mr. Douglas," said Inspector McPher-son. "They're new ones to us, but we have great hopes they're a pair we've been wanting for a long time, but couldn't put our hands on— We'll get them on the question of the car that was seen, if you will tell me the number of their car."

"There they are now," said John, scarcely managing to control the excitement in his voice.

"The tall man, and the blonde in the russet coat." The two detectives moved off, and the rest of the little party huddled in their wake. When the couple saw them, Nellie casually moved away, Slippery Sam looked quickly round, hesitated, then stopped.

"Mr. Burton-Ware?" said McPherson, and Slippery Sam said:

"Yes, but who—"

"I believe you have an Armstrong-Siddeley BLO 480?" interrupted McPherson deliberately.

"I think there's some mistake," said Burton-Ware coldly, and suddenly lifting his right fist he crashed it into McPherson's jaw, turned, and ran. It was unfortunate for Slippery Sam that Sara happened to be just there, to stick out her foot and bring him heavily to the ground.

"No mistake here!" grinned Sergeant Coles as he slipped on the handcuffs.

EPILOGUE

THEY were all gathered, Vanessa, Caroline, Sara, and John, not to mention the great J. Johnston Phillimore himself, in the large airy office of Chief Inspector McPherson at Scotland Yard; and Sara was nearly gibbering with excitement. She had had a wonderful morning giving the most lurid and innaccurate accounts of their adventure to admiring and sympathetic reporters, until Caroline had spoilt her fun by intruding the cold breath of truth. And now here she was, in Scotland Yard itself, and not just in any old room either, but in the precincts sacred to no less a personage than the Chief Inspector. And J. Johnson Phillimore, a dry little man whose eyes disappeared when he smiled, had been murmuring that he had ideas about rewards for all of them; and now the Chief Inspector, as he always had done in Sara's dreams, was going on about how the Burton-Wares had been responsible for a great many robberies, but so cleverly that the C.I.D. couldn't discover, far less catch, the perpetrators, and what a great service the Storms and Douglases had done Scotland Yard. And the only annoying thing about it all, Sara felt, was that it was so marvellous, so thrilling and exciting, that she couldn't take it in properly.

"And," the Chief Inspector finished his recital of this most successful coup, and beamed on them,

"Scotland Yard has to thank you, and your holi-day in Switzerland for it all...."

"But actually," said Caroline, as, rather dazed, they came out into the sunshine of the Embank-ment, "Scotland Yard has to thank the school drains for it all."

THE END